DEATH
AT THE
OLIVE PRESS

1176-BONE

DEATH
AT THE
OLIVE PRESS

Ellen Boneparth

1176-BONE

Library of Congress Number:		00-190967
ISBN #:	Hardcover	0-7388-2033-4
	Softcover	0-7388-2034-2

To order additional copies of this book, contact:
Xlibris Corporation
1-888-7-XLIBRIS
www.Xlibris.com
Orders@Xlibris.com

CONTENTS

ACKNOWLEDGMENTS

In the exhilarating, challenging, and sometimes vexing, process of learning to write fiction, I have been blessed with guidance and support from many extraordinary women. First, Lesley Kellas Payne, independent fiction editor, wise, passionate, and compassionate friend; Alexis Masters, a writing soul sister who gave me her own name for Alexi; dear friends with whom I share writing and Greece—Mara Keller, Jane Chapman, Elissa Raffa, Carol Christ, Judy Logan, Jo Stuart, Eleni Fourtouni, Pat Felch, Melpo Troumbi. Thank you Elaine Vickery and Guy Campbell for the cover of this book.

I am also fortunate to have a wonderful circle of Greek friends—too many to name—who have made my time living in their country a joy. A special *evharisto* to Aphroditi Vavouyios who gave me my love of the Greek language and her loving friendship; to the Athens circle; to the Lesbos circle; and to the Aegina circle, with special thanks to the Kouros family.

Over the last twenty years, I have shared Greece with many women taking part in the International Women's Studies Institute. To Judy Mings, in memoriam, to Lily Cincone, and to the participants in IWSI programs from around the world, thank you for enriching my life.

To my Santa Rosa writers' group, thank you for providing invaluable criticism and a supportive environment in which to grow.

Most of all, to my husband, Jim Wilkinson, who made the olive press a reality and who believes in me even more than I believe in myself.

SERROS

CHAPTER 1

Church bells clanged harshly. She scrambled up the steep, rocky path from the olive press to the ancient temple. Panting, she collapsed at the temple site on the mountaintop. Shattered white marble columns. Bodies of goats, cats, dogs, crushed under huge stones. Mounds of bloodied fur . . .

Alexis awoke with a start, fighting her way out of the nightmare that had plagued her since Easter. She stared at the clock face. Too early. She needed more sleep but the dream might return. She lay back, breathed slowly, deeply. The heat, dry, parching, spurred her to get up and water the garden before the unusually early heat wave took its toll.

She gave herself her accustomed speech. Alexis Davidov, get a hold of yourself. It's June. You're in Greece, nesting on your beloved island of Serros, living in the olive press, the *liotrivi*, your dream house. For six months, you've been fighting to make this happen. You will not let anyone take it away.

She reached for a tee shirt and shorts on the straight-backed chair. In the small, rustic bathroom, she doused her face, gulped spring water from the jug, wove her chestnut hair into a braid.

She crossed the dark, main room of the olive press, stepped outside, the kittens scampering after her onto the flagstones. In the gray light, she surveyed her garden: coral, pink and white geraniums in round clay pots, rough stone table and benches, traditional beehive stone oven, herb and vegetable plot. All as it should be, blending with the centuries-old stone terraces and bountiful olive trees gracing the mountainside.

Except the smell. Alexis sniffed the air. Faintly acrid, like a

dying hearth. She checked the stone oven, even though it had
been days since she'd used it. Nothing. She flicked a cinder from
her skin. No, just dirt.

The early morning stillness was shattered by the rapid tolling
of the bell from the village church in Pygi. Insistent ringing, a
hurried beat. Was it a local saint's day she didn't know about?
Damn, no phone; she'd been waiting for months. If the bell didn't
stop soon, she'd have to drive down to the village to investigate.

As she began to water, she spotted someone on the path.

Popi, urging on her ragged donkey, shouted, "What are you
doing, girl? Don't you know about the fire?"

"Oh, God. The church bell. I smelled fire, but I—Is the
fire in Pygi?"

"Not too far away. I came to get you." Popi wiped the dirt
from her face with the ends of her kerchief. "Alexi, right now the
fire's moving slowly, but that could change. You've got to track it."

Without a phone?

Popi seemed to read her mind. "Girl, you can't stay here. You're
alone on the hillside. Close up the house. Go down to the harbor."

Mercifully, the ringing stopped.

"Leave?" Alexis said. "That's not what you're doing."

"The house is all we've got. But we know how to fight fires.
We've done it before."

"How?"

"With wet brooms. We beat the flames. You put water in containers all around the house."

"I can do that. I'm not abandoning the *liotrivi*, not now anyway." Alexis tightened. "The cats. They can't wander around free.
Will you keep them for me?"

"Bring them. If you hear the church bell again, come immediately to Pygi."

Popi flicked the donkey's side with her switch and was off.
Alexis bolted into action. She brought every conceivable water con-
tainer outside, placed them at strategic locations, filled them with
the hose. She had only one broom, wondered if there were others

to be had in the village. Not likely. She knew the tenacious people of Pygi. Every available soul would beat at the flames until the last moment.

Could it really happen? Could the olive press go up in flames? Losing the *liotrivi* now, after months of struggle, would be a crushing blow. Her despicable neighbors, the Koutsos cousins, would rejoice she was gone. She couldn't accept that. Not after she'd stood up to them for so long.

Early on, Alexis had pumped Popi about the absentee owners of the orchards that bordered the olive press. They were bad people, Popi had said. Loukas Koutsos, vulgar and a braggart, bald and obese, had somehow managed to snare a young wife with all the money he'd made as an accountant in Athens.

No one knew what Panayiotis, the younger, handsome cousin, did, but occasionally he came back to the island to show off his flashy clothes and gold chains. He'd never hidden his anger that his cousin, Loukas, inherited buildable land below the press, and his cousin, Andonis, got the building, while he ended up with land above the path, too steep to build on.

Bad people was an understatement, Alexis muttered to herself. The two cousins, crude and ugly in the beginning, had become sadistic. For six months they'd harassed her in every way they could think of, making her life a misery.

Alexis loaded the cats in the van, headed down the hill. In Pygi, she spotted Popi's husband, Thanos, his swarthy skin livid with exertion, tearing back and forth from his truck to the spring. She found Popi at home, kneeling beside a carved wood dowry chest, hurriedly packing up her hand-embroidered linens.

"Alexi, put the cats in the pantry," Popi said. "Then call Helen in Nemea."

"Thanks. You're a blessing."

Helen picked up immediately. "Alexi, are you all right?"

"My broom is at the ready, but I'm not sure I can do this alone."

"You're not alone. Yiannis and Theo are leaving for Serros right away. There's no ferry, but they've arranged a speedboat."

"Theo?" she blurted out. "I thought he was in Albania."

"He came back a couple of days ago." Despite the anxiety of the moment, Alexis broke into a grin.

"Wait," Helen said. "My dear husband wants to talk."

"Alexi *mou*," Yiannis barked, "don't panic."

"I'm not—exactly. Should I be?"

"This damn heat wave. I spoke to the fire service. The fire's following the southern shoreline rather than climbing the mountain. That's good. But if it reaches the east side of the island, it will race your way through the break in the mountains. Here, Helen wants to get back on."

"Alexi, pack your van with your most precious things. Be at the harbor at one to pick up Yiannis and Theo."

"Helen, this is above and beyond—"

"Alexi *mou*, you're our *koumbara*, Christina's godmother. Now go pack."

Alexis met Thanos in the yard as he carried pails of water from the shed. "We've saved this village before," he panted, "but you, a woman, alone up there?"

"I have help coming."

"A man, I hope."

The perennial chauvinism. "Yes. My friend Yiannis from Nemea."

"Okay, then. Good luck to you."

Alexis needed luck; she also needed help. Although she wouldn't have admitted it six months ago, she couldn't manage alone. The olive press seemed determined to teach her that.

*   *   *

Alexis waited on the deserted pier as the speedboat hurtled into Serros harbor. With word of the fire, visitors had scurried to leave, and locals were staying close to their radios and telephones.

Yiannis, heftier than ever, his pipe clenched in his mouth, lumbered off the boat, armed with a chainsaw and pick. Theo gracefully jumped out after him, carrying another chainsaw, a shovel and two brooms. They were sopping wet from the spray.

Yiannis kissed Alexis on both cheeks. "To work."

She suddenly felt awkward, not sure how to greet Theo, her former workman and daily companion. A kiss would be too intimate; a handshake, too formal. She squeezed his arm, reached for one of the shovels.

He grinned, clucked his tongue against his teeth to negate her offer of help. "Good to see you, Alexi."

They headed briskly down the pier to the van. Yiannis drove with a seeming sense of urgency.

"Yianni, what about the fire-fighting planes?" Alexis asked.

"Fully occupied elsewhere. They'll come to Serros only if a village is threatened. Don't worry. Theo and I have a plan. We'll clear a section of land next to the *liotrivi*. If the fire starts up the hillside, the fire break should keep it from reaching the house."

"You're going to cut down Loukas' olive trees?"

"One row, just enough to make the fire break."

"He'll go crazy when he finds out. What if he and Panayiotis show up?" Alexis could just imagine the confrontation—shouting, menacing moves, potential violence.

"We'll finish before they know we're here," Theo said.

As soon as they pulled up to the press, the two men grabbed the chain saws, went at the trees closest to the building with fierce determination. Alexis, ears covered against the shrill whines, watched with sadness as olive trees crashed to the ground. She'd have to compensate Loukas for his losses, but the cost would be less than rebuilding the *liotrivi*.

Theo, dripping with sweat, waved an empty bottle at Alexis who went inside to re-fill the water bottles. Coming back around the house, she caught the view of the sea, wider, grander than before. It always went that way in her dealings with Loukas—dirt turned into gold.

The air had thickened. It smelled bitter like charred meat. While Yiannis took a break inside, Theo began digging a trench.

"The most dangerous thing about olive trees," he said, "is the extensive root system. The flames travel down the inside of the trunk and fan out along the roots underground. The fire can pop out again, far from the tree. This trench will help, but we've got to keep close watch once the fire gets here."

She grabbed a shovel, tried for optimism. "Maybe it won't come this way."

"It will, Alexi. The wind has shifted."

She knew he was right. The wind was now blowing from the east, strengthening by the minute. The olive trees quivered, the young ones bending gracefully in the gusts.

"What do we do after the trench?" she asked.

"Move the furniture away from the doors and windows. Then we rest and wait for the fire."

*   *   *

Yiannis and Theo had piled Alexis' furnishings in the middle of the living room, covered them with blankets, bound them with rope. Now, exhausted, the two men slept sprawled on couch pillows on the floor. It would be a long night.

Sitting by the kitchen window, Alexis scrutinized the hillside in the fading light. Like ballet dancers, the trees arched in the wind. A loud crack outside the kitchen window made her jump.

Her heart pounding, she leaned out the window. A heavy gust tore through the branches, rattled the shutters. A tree limb swung wildly like a skeleton in the wind.

There was something noxious in the air.

Time to stand guard outside. She looked in on the men. They needed time to recover, but the fire would wait for no one.

*   *   *

It came fast. The three of them felt the fire before they saw it. A hot rush of wind buffeted them. Feathery ash and cinders fell on their faces and clothing. Their nostrils burned. Then, in the dark, they glimpsed an eerie orange glow a hundred meters below.

The fire moved gracefully, steadily, up the stone terraces, like a lady in a crimson and gold evening gown ascending a grand staircase. The thin leaves and branches of the younger trees ignited like sparklers. The fire charred the ropey trunks of the older trees before gliding up to the next terrace.

Alexis moaned softly. "Some of those trees are a hundred years old."

Yiannis clasped her shoulder. "Most will come back."

"Over there," Theo shouted. "Below the cistern. Alexi, stay back."

The men dashed over, began beating at flames on the ground with wet brooms. Alexis couldn't simply watch. With her broom, she chased angrily after sparks in the air.

Loud pops. Trees burst into flame at the other end of Loukas' property. They tore over to the new outbreak. The fire seemed thicker, more menacing, but they kept up with it, getting better at their task. Theo attacked licks of flame on the ground; Yiannis shoveled earth to smother them; Alexis stamped down the earth, watched for rogue flames.

It went like that for several hours, the three of them sweating heavily, moving up and down the trench, beating back the flames. The heat was brutal, searing, penetrating the soles of Alexis' hiking boots, making her eyes, nose, and throat burn. She had no time to feel afraid—except in one brief respite when it hit her that, alone, she would have been lost.

Had the fire reached Pygi? She hadn't heard the church bell over the howling wind and cracking trees. She suspected the villagers were lined up outside their houses, anxiously waiting to do battle.

The flames seemed to be searching for higher ground. They had a brief respite as the fire stormed up the mountainside above the press, apparently crossing the mountain path to Panayiotis' property. Then flames shot out of the ground next to her side window. Yiannis and Theo attacked the new outbreak angrily as if the fire had played a trick by bursting out behind them. Arms and shoulders aching, Alexis swung her broom at the sparks, beautiful, deadly, fireflies.

Around midnight, the wind suddenly shifted. The whooshing sound of the fire dropped to a sibilant rustling. The flames vanished as if the crimson and gold lady of the evening had retired. Loukas' orchard smoldered in the dark, the ghostly trees smoking from inside their trunks. It was a bizarre scene, other-worldly.

Yiannis wiped Alexis' face with his handkerchief, and, grinning, pulled out his pipe. "That's it for now, although we need to keep watch. Is there any food?"

She grinned back, went inside, collected the makings for sandwiches. They spread out a cloth, dropped to the ground. Ravenous, bodies aching, they drifted into contentment—the plan had worked. Yiannis leaned back against the house, half-closed his eyes.

Theo, seemingly restless, circled the building. "Another shift in the wind could bring the fire back before we know it. I'll stay out here. You two go sleep."

"I'm too keyed-up to sleep," Alexis said.

When Yiannis retired inside, Alexis remained on the ground, a towel over her shoulders, listening to the hissing of the dying fire. There was a delicious ripple of cool air that made her skin tingle. Cool air—she'd never again take it for granted. She didn't try to engage Theo in conversation. Small talk seemed irrelevant; expressions of gratitude would be brushed off. She stayed to share a companionable silence.

Periodically, Theo paced up and down. Once he found a patch of ground burning from cinders which he doused with the hose. He led Alexis to the north end of the building. "See up the valley there? The red glow? We need to keep an eye on that in case the wind changes again."

"I will, Theo. Please rest. You must be dead."

"I'll lie down on the deck chair out here. I can smell trouble in my sleep. You go in now."

Alexis gave his hand a gentle squeeze. "Okay, but I'm getting you a pillow. Please don't give me any speeches about how you've slept in worse places."

*   *   *

At dawn, they woke to the roar of motors overhead, rushed outside. Planes flew up the valley to drop their loads of sea water on the remaining flames.

"That's it, Alexi," Yiannis said.

The enormity of what they'd done finally hit her—they'd saved her home. "I'm speechless. How to tell you two—"

"Alexi, you wielded that broom like a true Greek," Theo said.

Yiannis roared. "You look like one, too, with your hair tied up in that scarf and dirt all over your face."

"Fine with me."

He yawned. "I say we rest until noon. Then Theo and I will move the furniture back and catch the afternoon ferry to Nauplion."

"Not before I treat to a big fish lunch at the harbor."

"Not fish. I'm sure the fishermen stayed home to fight the fire. But lunch, yes, with pleasure."

Inside, they washed up in turn. The men returned to their pillows on the floor.

In the bedroom, Alexis closed her eyes, but couldn't sleep. At ten, she rose, put on clean clothes, and made coffee. Her hair smelled of smoke, her hands had started to blister.

Theo joined her in the kitchen.

"I keep wondering what it's like out there," she whispered. "Would you like to make a survey after we drink our coffee?"

He nodded. "We were lucky, Alexi."

"Luck had something to do with it. Aeolus smiled on us. Friends had more to do with it. It seems you continue to save me from disaster."

He grinned. "My pleasure."

They tiptoed past the snoring Yiannis. It was a shock to step out into the flowering garden, untouched by the flames, then look down the hill at the black skeletons of olive trees.

"Let's climb the path to the temple," Theo proposed. "We'll get the best view from there."

Alexis had not walked up the path since that terrible day at Easter. Now was the time to get over her aversion. She gritted her teeth, followed his lead.

A hundred meters above the press, they found a few of Panayiotis' trees scorched. The rest of his land was untouched.

"Panayiotis was luckier than his cousin," Alexis said. "I'd say Loukas' property has dropped in value. I'm not sorry for him, but I am for the trees."

They turned back. Near the house, Alexis glanced down the hill, strained her eyes for a good look. "What's that mound down there? Someone sleeping?" she half-joked, darting off.

"Oh, my God. Theo," she screamed. "Theo."

He came running.

She clutched his arm. "It's a body. Christ, a body."

He pulled her behind him as if to shield her. "Step back. You don't have to look."

Alexis stared, transfixed. The body, face down, had been wrapped in a sheet which the fire had scorched, blackening the clothes of the victim. Theo rolled the corpse over with his foot.

From its girth, Alexis had already guessed. "It's Loukas, isn't it?" she croaked, hugging herself with her arms.

"He must have been here when the fire came up the mountain."

Alexis finally turned away. "Lie down in the path of a fire?"

"He wasn't conscious, maybe not even alive. His head's been bashed in. Alexi, come." Theo took her firmly by the elbow, guided her back down the path to the *liotrivi*.

Yiannis lounged on the garden bench, smoking his pipe. "Good morning, comrades."

Alexis stumbled over. "Yianni—" She choked up. "Yianni, we found Loukas' body—badly burned—below in the orchard." She gagged, staggered to the edge of the garden and heaved, gagged more.

Theo came over, held her. "Come sit, Alexi. I'll bring you water."

"No. Inside." She lunged for the front door, huddled in an armchair, a hand covering her mouth.

Still confused, Yiannis pulled a chair up beside her. "Loukas was fighting the fire by himself?"

"No, he was bludgeoned. His body was wrapped in a sheet and left to burn. How could anyone do such a thing?"

Yiannis leaned closer. "Murdered?"

"Had to be. His head was crushed."

"Alexi, this is bad for you."

"For me?" she moaned. "Why?"

"If he was murdered—"

"How could I possibly kill Loukas? He's three times my size."

Alexis caught Yiannis staring at Theo.

"You could with help," Yiannis said.

"Oh, no. I had the same—I didn't want to think it."

She lurched over to Theo who was leaning against the wall. "You've got to get out of here. Cross the mountain like the Albanian boys who fixed the path. We'll send your friend, Vassilis, to pick you up in his boat." She shook him. "Theo, you've got to leave. Now."

Theo looked angry. "Why should I run away?"

"You know. You can't be connected to any of this. It'd be too easy to accuse you."

He fixed his gaze on her. "What about you?"

"I'm an American. I've got the U.S. Embassy. It's completely different for an Albanian. Please."

Yiannis stepped over to Theo, gripped his arm. "She's right. Go back to Nauplion with the fisherman. We'll swear you never left Nemea."

Theo still hesitated, stubbornness firming his features.

She saw he wanted to stay for her. She had to make him escape. "Theo, if you care about me, please go. You're the only way they can link me to the murder. Without an accomplice, I couldn't be guilty."

He looked at her intensely, held her face in his hands for a long moment, then slipped silently out. Alexis closed the door behind him, clutched the knob to stop trembling.

Yiannis pulled her back to the armchair. "That was good, what you said. He never would have left otherwise."

"Oh, God. Yianni, what are we going to do?"

Yiannis searched his pockets for his pipe. "We're going to take a few minutes, work on our story. Then, we'll go down to Popi's, contact the fisherman, and call the police."

PIRAEUS

CHAPTER 2

Through the high window of her cell, Alexis gazed longingly at the blue and white Greek flag, billowing in the summer sunshine. She pictured sailboats with rainbow-colored spinnakers skimming across the cobalt blue Saronic Gulf. This was crazy. Better not to imagine life beyond the walls.

The Greek authorities had pointedly refused to call it a cell. A lock-up with a private lavatory, they'd said, as if she weren't really in jail. Whatever euphemism they used, Alexis thought angrily, it was a prison and she was being held against her will. From Saturday evening when the Serros constable had delivered Loukas' body to the morgue until now—thirty-six hours—she'd been incarcerated without being charged.

The worst part was the smell. The small room reeked of cigarette smoke which had penetrated the cracks in the tea-colored walls and linoleum, the mattress stuffing, the stained white plastic of the chair and table. Hundreds of prisoners must have chain-smoked cigarette after cigarette, waiting for something to happen.

She had to get out of there. She crossed to the steel door, peered through the filthy pane of glass. Soon the sullen matron would grudgingly bring her a tepid cup of instant coffee.

Yesterday morning, investigators had questioned her about the enmity between her and Loukas. She'd answered openly—she had nothing to hide. She was a victim, not a perpetrator. *Loukas* had harassed *her*.

The police simply couldn't understand that. She should have left his corpse to rot instead of calling them. She felt like kicking something.

Surely, Loukas had enemies; he was such a crude human being. The incompetent police should be searching for the real killer.
Loukas' devious business partner, for example. Instead, they'd fix-
ated on Theo, who, as far as the police knew, hadn't even been in
Serros during the fire.

She had to face it: there was more to this than her relations
with Loukas. Theo was Albanian. Even though Greek Albanian,
with a legal work permit, he was suspect by virtue of nationality,
guilty by association with all the illegal Albanian immigrants in
Greece.

Alexis, too, was a foreigner, seemingly under suspicion because
she'd chosen to live in Serros. The police couldn't conceive of a
"rich" *Americana* choosing to live on a remote Greek island. It
didn't matter that she was established in Greece—had many Greek
friends, an outstanding record at the Lincoln American School,
had used her modest inheritance to purchase property. She must
have a surreptitious reason for living in Serros. The police seemed
determined to hold her until they figured it out.

Thank God she had her lawyers, Maria and Nikos Antonides.
She'd liked them from their first meeting back in February. Maria,
petite, feminine, almost doll-like, was the sharp legal strategist,
while serious-looking Nikos, in his vest and horn-rimmed glasses,
acted as the sympathetic counselor. Rushing back from a weekend
in the country when they'd heard Alexis was at the detention center, they'd put a stop to all questioning, had immediately drawn
up a petition for her release.

Alexis picked up her watch from the plastic table. Seven- thirty,
a.m. When would Maria and Nikos arrive? Being dependent was
infuriating. She couldn't even make a long distance phone call to
Sophia in Serros, or Helen in Nemea, to reassure them she was
okay. What reassurance could she give, anyway? Only that she was
alive, unharmed, as yet uncharged.

No. She wouldn't become defeatist. She had to concentrate,
get out from under the black cloud of suspicion seeded by Loukas'
family. It was insanity. In the last six months, she'd gone from

being a passionate philhellene, eager to sink roots into the soil of the country she loved, to a suspected murderer.

People had often asked why she'd moved to Greece. In part, because there was nothing for her in America. After her parents' angry divorce when she was thirteen, her father had abandoned her, remarried a woman only a few years older than Alexis who had three young kids. Alexis had been crushed, but hid her pain from her mother who tried valiantly to give her daughter a normal life.

Mother and daughter had only four more years together, painful years marked by a diagnosis of breast cancer, surgery, chemotherapy. When her mother died in Alexis' last year of high school, Alexis felt adrift. Her hometown, San Diego, once a sunny playground, filled her with a sense of loss. She coped the only way she could— by building a thick protective shell, letting few people come close out of fear they, too, would leave her.

The key ground in the lock of her cell. The matron, her face pinched like a rodent's, barged in with the breakfast tray.

Alexis squeezed the bread. For the second morning, it was rock hard. "Is there anything else? Biscuits?"

"This is not a hotel." The matron swung around, banging her metal tray against the steel door.

Not a hotel. Alexis dunked the bread in the coffee. Prison work must attract sadists.

When had her sad, young life started to turn around? College. She'd moved as far from San Diego as possible, to Boston University where, influenced by her mother's practicality, she'd prepared for a career teaching high school social studies. Yet, Alexis also had an artistic side that needed nourishment. She indulged her passion for art and archeology by taking a minor in art history.

For four years, she'd relished the intellectual atmosphere and vast array of museums in Boston, but suffered through the chill, dreary winters. Her close friendship with Helen, her roommate since freshman year, had gotten her through the times when she was overcome by a sense of isolation, loss, fear of the future.

Greece had been their high adventure together. They'd spent

a month as volunteers on a dig directed by Petros, who never noticed Alexis then, but later came into her life as friend and lover.
She and Helen traveled through the islands, free spirits soaking up
sun, hiking to far-flung villages, dancing with old men in *tavernas*,
flirting with the young ones.

After their island tour, Helen had rushed back to Yiannis, the
foreman on the dig. Her summer romance had turned serious. She
decided to remain in Greece and urged Alexis to join her.

For Alexis, Greece had become a different kind of love affair.
She'd found a degree of spontaneity in human relations and a joy
in life she'd never experienced anywhere else. The renowned Greek
sea and sunshine, rugged terrain smelling of wild oregano and
thyme, piercing white light and blood orange sunsets, village
women pulling strangers into their homes for coffee and sweets. It
had all been irresistible.

From the first, life in Athens had charmed her. It was a friend-
lier, less crowded city then, a city that always had time for gossip
in a sidewalk cafe. A linguist, speaking French and German, she
mastered Greek quickly. Alexis adopted the softer name of Alexi
(even if typically used for males), dropping the "s" as Greeks did
when addressing someone. While she still carried her shell on her
back, she'd nonetheless basked in the warming sun, more secure
every year knowing she could take care of herself, find joy in a new
beginning.

Alexis took a sip of the watery Nescafe, pushed it away.

In the past year something had gone terribly wrong, starting
with her relationship with Petros. It had been a boon at first. She'd
attended lectures and conferences with him, mixed eagerly with
his students and colleagues. She'd been filled with admiration for
the innovative archeologist until she'd seen his personal life up
close.

Petros' mother, Diana Diamandopoulos, an extremely wealthy
woman, widowed early, desperately desired the continuation of
the family line. At the same time, she wanted Petros, her only
child, to herself. Since she could have both only by dominating

her future daughter-in-law, she hunted for spineless creatures for Petros to marry.

Alexis and Diana had had a strained relationship from the start, but Alexis' issue wasn't with mother, but son. Petros resisted Diana on small things but followed her lead when making major decisions, exactly opposite from the way Alexis thought he should behave.

She felt her lower back muscles tightening, a familiar reaction to stress. She lay down to do leg stretches. The thin mattress caved in at the middle. She should lie on something hard, but the floor of the cell was too dirty. She stretched out as best she could, slowly brought one knee, then the other, toward her chest.

The Oxford fellowship made Alexis see the light. Just before Christmas, Petros had phoned to say he'd decided not to go to England for the spring term.

Alexis had been mystified. "How can that be? Teaching at Oxford? It's the opportunity of a lifetime."

"Perhaps, but Diana needs me to help remodel the villa."

"Diana's an interior designer."

"All the same, she needs a second opinion."

Alexis exploded. "That's bullshit, and you know it. She just wants you under her thumb. She kept you living at home until she could find the right apartment for you, a half-block from her house. Now this."

"Alexi, you don't understand Greek culture. Children don't abandon their parents."

She fumed. "What I understand is you're a victim of emotional blackmail and unable to do a thing about it."

After that, their relations had gone downhill fast. Petros retaliated by ridiculing the olive press. He'd been against her buying it, was offended when she took a leave of absence from school to do the restoration. Although they could have easily continued seeing each other on weekends once she'd moved to Serros, they kept finding excuses not to.

Restless, she got up again, tossed back her long hair, clasped her hands in front of her and twisted from side to side. Then, perched on the edge of the plastic chair, she rotated her head to loosen the muscles knotting at the back of her neck and across her bony shoulders. She began to relax.

Almost nine on her watch. Maria and Nikos would arrive any minute to spring her.

*   *   *

Within the hour, the matron banged on the cell door. "Visitor. Come."

Alexis straightened her shoulders, tucked her tee shirt into her jeans. Maria and Nikos at last. She followed the scowling matron down the dreary corridor to the consultation room.

It wasn't them. A young woman in her twenties, plump and freckled, in a seersucker suit and blouse, looked up from the file folder she'd been studying, dried her apparently sweaty hand on her skirt.

She jumped up. "I'm Elizabeth O'Donnell from the U.S. Embassy. You must be Alexis Davidov. I mean, I know you're Alexis Davidov. Who else would you be?"

"Unless there are lots of American women in here suspected of murder—"

"Oh, no, only you. Sorry, that didn't come out right. I'm a bit nervous. I've never done one of these visits before."

"That makes two of us." Alexis pulled out a chair, motioned to the young woman to sit. "What do you do at the Embassy?"

"Consular Section, American Citizen Services. Actually, I've just arrived in Greece. Everyone else is on vacation."

"Where are my lawyers?"

"I don't know. I didn't see anyone outside." The consular officer re-opened her file, seemed to review her notes. "So, how have you been treated, Ms. Davidov?"

"To what exactly are you referring? I'm being held without a charge. I don't know why the police are detaining me or how long this will go on."

O'Donnell flushed; sweat stains had spread under her arms. "It must be terrible, but what I mean is . . ." She examined her notes. "Have you been able to see your lawyer? Have you been allowed to make phone calls? Are you being treated the same as Greek prisoners?"

"I have no idea. I haven't seen any Greek prisoners. I spoke with my lawyers yesterday. I'm expecting them any minute. I can make local phone calls."

"Good. Is there anything I can do for you?"

"You could get me out of here."

"Oh, dear. I really wish I could." She twisted her hands, then looked determined. "I don't know if I'm allowed to say this, but I'd be happy to call someone in the States for you."

Alexis felt a pang of sadness. "Look, I don't mean to be difficult. I appreciate your concern. As for the States, my mother's dead and I'm estranged from my father."

"Well, do you need anything? Food? Toothbrush?"

"What do you mean you can't get me out of here?"

"This is an internal Greek matter."

"I'm an American citizen. I presume that's why you're here, not to sell toothbrushes."

O'Donnell giggled nervously. "You have quite a sense of humor. Ms. Davidov, here's my number at work. Wait, let me also write down my home phone. If they harass you in any way, please let me know."

The young woman was trying, but the visit was a joke.

"How long can they hold a foreign national without charging her?" Alexis said.

"I don't know. Maybe I can research that and get back to you tomorrow."

"I don't expect to be here tomorrow."

"Oh. Good." The young woman looked relieved, shook Alexis' hand, and signaled for the matron.

*   *   *

Back in her cell, Alexis slumped onto the cot. She checked her watch again. Past noon. She'd better call Maria and Nikos.

As she sat up, a muscle spasm pierced her lower back. Not now, she prayed. She gingerly raised herself and shuffled over to the door. "*Parakalo*," she called through the door. "Please. *Parakalo*."

The matron came to the window, raised her pencil-thin eyebrows in a question.

"I must phone my lawyers. They're supposed to be here for a meeting."

"No meeting now."

"You don't understand. We have a meeting scheduled. I must find out where they are."

"No meeting. In detention, only one visit a day."

"What?"

"Only one visit. The rules."

"You didn't tell me that," Alexis thundered.

The matron shrugged.

"Okay. Now I know. Now I absolutely must speak with my lawyers on the phone."

"Too late. Tomorrow morning." The matron turned to leave.

Alexis was desperate. "If you take me to the phone, I'll pay you as soon as I get my wallet back."

The woman looked back at her slyly, held up ten fingers. Ten thousand drachma—an outrageous amount. Suppressing her fury, Alexis nodded.

The cell door swung open. She hobbled down the corridor, her back throbbing, to the phone on the wall, dialed urgently. "Nikos? It's Alexis. Why didn't you come?"

"We were there a couple of hours ago, Alexi, but you had a visitor."

"Some silly creature from the US Embassy. They didn't tell me I can have only one visitor a day."

"You can always see your lawyer, but only one visitor at a time. Try to keep anyone from coming when we're expected."

"I didn't invite this woman. She showed up. Nikos, am I going to have to stay here?"

"Unfortunately. They won't act on our petition until they've reviewed the autopsy report. Maria was down at the coroner's office all morning. There's something strange going on."

"What do you mean?"

"We've been assuming Loukas died from a blow to the head. They may have found something else. We'll know tomorrow, Wednesday at the latest."

Alexis didn't speak. She didn't want Nikos to know she was crying.

"Alexi?"

"Are they looking for the murderer? Checking Loukas' associates? His slimy partner?"

"They are and we are, Alexi. The partner seems to have skipped town. That's promising, suggests he's hiding something. We'll find him." He paused. An uncomfortable silence. "There's one other thing, Alexi. The police have found a witness who claims Theo was in Serros the day of the fire. An old woman says she saw him at the harbor."

"My God. What do we do?"

"Nothing. The old woman's testimony has to be weighed against our witnesses who swear Theo was in Nemea. I tell you only because it may give the police a reason to hold you longer. You, of course, will not discuss Theo with anyone."

"Of course not," she whispered into the phone.

"Alexi, Georgia will visit you this evening. Can you hold on until then?"

Georgia, Petros' fabulous aunt. She and Alexis had become terrific friends as soon as Alexis started seeing Petros; they'd stayed close through the winter.

"My sciatica's kicking up. Please ask Georgia to bring muscle relaxers."

"Anything else?"

"Ten thousand drachma."

"Got it. There's one other message—from Helen. She said you're
not to blame yourself. This has nothing to do with Serros or the
olive press."

Helen knew her so well. If not for Helen, there might not have
been an olive press. Everyone in Athens had told her she was crazy.
Petros had assured her that, as a foreigner, she'd be cheated at
every turn. Even Georgia had urged her to wait until she got a
good engineer to oversee the job. Not Helen. She'd given the project
her whole-hearted support.

"Nikos, the matron is gesturing. I'd better go."

Alexis made her way back to her cell, holding the wall for
support. She checked her watch for the tenth time that day. How
was she going to get through the afternoon? She had to do something more than wait.

What? Perhaps make a written record of her battles with Loukas
and Panayiotis. Not even battles—skirmishes. It all seemed so petty,
a vendetta by greedy neighbors, a ridiculous but necessary court
case. Yet it ended with a corpse and suspicion of murder.

Helen's phone message came back to her: don't blame yourself. Okay. She'd tough out the next day, possibly two, without
collapsing into self-recrimination. But Helen was wrong about one
thing—her plight had everything to do with Serros and the olive
press.

CHAPTER 3

Monday evening brought a new matron—pimply face, vermilion lips, brassy hair held in place by a gaudy gold headband. "Mrs. Diamandopoulos is waiting."

Despite her best efforts to relax, Alexis was prostrated by lower back pain. "I can't get up. Can you bring the visitor in here?"

"Against the rules."

"What difference does it make? You can watch through the door."

"Impossible. You must come with me."

Alexis slowly rolled onto her side. Changing positions was the horror of sciatica. The sagging cot made it torture. The bedsprings creaked like a door on rusty hinges as she inched her legs over the metal rim. So far so good; pain, but no crippling spasm. She pushed up on her arm so her body made a forty-five degree angle with the bed, took several deep breaths.

The matron yanked Alexis by her free arm to a sitting position, making her prisoner howl in pain.

"You can't do that," Alexis yelled.

The matron blanched, taken aback. "What do you want me to do?"

"Stand in front of me. Help me up. Slowly."

The matron did as she was asked. The pain was so intense Alexis thought her legs would buckle. She stood, panting. "I can walk, but very slowly."

At the end of the corridor, Georgia caught sight of Alexis leaning on the matron, shambling down the hall. Georgia came running, her red mouth wide open in shock. "*Agapi mou*, what did they do to you?"

"This sometimes happens when I'm stressed. Fighting the fire might have triggered it. Did you bring muscle relaxers?"

"Several different kinds. Here. I'll get on the other side."

In the consultation room, Alexis said, "I can't sit. Please let me see the pills."

Georgia grasped the matron's arm, issued a command. "You will bring some water immediately. Then we'll discuss my niece's treatment." She ransacked her tote bag, held up three pill bottles.

Georgia was amazing, Alexis thought. A wise and gutsy woman who wanted to be called "aunt" and played the role perfectly.

"Thank goodness. You brought what I usually take. Two of those in the small bottle, please."

Alexis took the paper cup from the matron, downed the pills. "I can stand, but I need a tall, straight-backed chair to lean on."

One look from Georgia and the matron rushed off to find one. Georgia massaged the back of Alexis' neck. "How long before the pills take effect?"

"The spasm will start easing in a few minutes. If I treat this right, I should be okay in a day or two. I'm just glad you came."

Georgia held her hand, started to cry. "I'm sorry to be emotional. I've been holding it in. Alexi, you're so damn brave."

"And you're so damn wonderful. Now before our visit's up, tell me what's going on in the real world. How's Sounion?"

"Darling, I appreciate your asking about me, but we have to talk about you. I want to bring in another lawyer."

"Is it that serious?"

"I have no idea how serious it is. I never thought you'd be here this long. Now, I know I introduced you to Maria and Nikos when Loukas started harassing you, and I do think well of them—"

"So do I."

"But they've never handled a murder case. I want your permission to call Roussakis. He's the best criminal lawyer around."

"Has this become a murder case? I thought I was just being detained."

"Of course you are, but we have to get you out of here. Maria and Nikos are smart, young lawyers, but they don't have connections. This is Greece. I want Roussakis."

Alexis was tongue-tied.

"Alexi, I hope you're not worried about the money."

"It's not the money," Alexis lied. It wasn't *only* the money— she trusted Maria and Nikos.

The matron came over, pointed to her watch. Georgia pulled the woman closer. "I want you to bring my niece whatever she wants." She stuffed a wad of drachma notes into the matron's pocket. "This chair goes into her cell. Understood?"

The matron patted her pocket. "I'll be here until tomorrow morning."

"Good. Alexi, how are you feeling now?"

Alexis moved her hands away from the chair, took a few hesitant steps. "I'm ambulatory. I need a pillow to put under my back in bed."

"I'll get you one," the matron said, scurrying away.

"Alexi, Petros called. He wants to know if he should come up from Messenia."

"That's kind of him, but I don't think he could do anything."

Georgia sighed. "Oh, Alexi, I wish you two—"

"Aunt Georgia, Petros and I really cared for each other, but he was never able to be with just me. I so much wanted him to be part of Serros. You know, I invited him to join us at Easter, but he chose to go to Diana's."

"I'd hoped you'd pull my engaging nephew away from her influence."

"I can't pull him. He has to want to leave."

Georgia gently enfolded Alexis in her arms and whispered in her ear. "Darling, think about Roussakis and call me whenever you can. I'll bring anything you need."

The matron led Alexis slowly down the hall. She eased onto the cot, her heart pounding. Georgia obviously thought she'd be tried for murder. Was she wrong to stick with Maria and Nikos?

They were her friends; they cared about her. But what if they couldn't handle a murder trial?

She reached for the bottle of pills. One more might bring on sleep.

*   *   *

The next morning, Alexis slowly pushed herself up, intensely relieved. The throbbing pain of the night before had diminished to a dull ache. Six a.m. She'd slept through the night. Wonder drugs.

She picked up the pillow she'd been lying on, cautiously stepped over to the straight chair. With the pillow behind her, she had enough support to sit and write. She was going to get the story of the olive press down. Somewhere in it lay the clues to what had happened.

She smiled weakly, remembering the day of discovery. She'd persuaded Petros to lead her students from the Lincoln American School on an excursion. He'd chosen the ancient temple on Serros, a rugged island only ninety minutes by hydrofoil from Piraeus harbor. Without beaches or tourist attractions, Serros was visited only by hardy foreigners and a few Greeks rejecting the beaten track.

The morning had been cold and blustery. They took taxis to Pygi, then led the kids up the rocky mountain path. The site at the top confused the kids. All they saw was the small, whitewashed chapel—old, not ancient. Petros pointed out the huge stones of the temple foundation underneath the chapel. The kids were distinctly unimpressed until he challenged them with the temple mystery. Petros at his best.

"This has been classified as a temple to Poseidon, god of the sea," he said, "because an ancient text mentions such a structure on Serros. Not likely. You can't even see this site from the sea. I think the temple belongs to a different deity. Can you guess who?"

Melinda, her spiky hairdo holding stiffly in the wind, looked smug. "Athena. Look at all the olive trees."

"No way." Steve, Alexis' most precocious student, yawned. "Those trees aren't big enough."

Petros nodded. "Other ideas?"

The kids sat stumped. Drops began to fall. Petros was oblivious. "What did the ancient Greeks do in the mountains?" he said. "They hunted. So, which deity?"

Finally, Isabel waved her chubby hand. "Artemis, protector of animals, goddess of the hunt."

At that moment, as if enraged by the loss of his temple, Poseidon unleashed a downpour. The kids ran to the path, bleated like sheep as they slid down the slick rocks. Steve took off ahead, dashed back to lead the group to shelter—a low-slung, stone structure with a broken tile roof. The kids huddled under the eaves, squealing with every crack of thunder.

To distract her charges, Alexis shoved the rotting door of the building inward. Peering into the gloom, she glimpsed strange machines, iron implements and decaying bags dangling from the roof beams, a large ominous vice. A towering millstone stood ready to roll around its basin, a leather harness draped on the center pole. She smelled the sour odor of a beast of burden that had plodded round the dirt floor. Rusting oil cans, funnels, measures, and ceramic jars were heaped next to a crumbling stone oven. It quickly came to her—an olive press, cornerstone of traditional Greek life.

Ankle deep in crunchy olive pits, she crossed to a small back room in complete disrepair. A window opening with a rotting wood frame admitted rays of light. Gingerly, Alexis leaned out, then gasped in pleasure.

Petros came up behind her. "Not a bad view. West, same as the temple."

"One of the most beautiful views I've seen."

"You're overcome by the electricity in the air. Listen, the rain's let up. We'd better go."

As Alexis herded the kids out, she spotted a plank of weath-

ered wood leaning against the millstone. *For sale* in faded blue
paint and an Athens phone number.

From that October day, Alexis had never looked back, even
though Loukas' deceitfulness over the sale of the press should have
warned her. Still, if Loukas hadn't tried to trick his cousin,
Andonis . . .

Alexis had located Andonis Koutsos, the owner of the olive
press, in a hole-in-the-wall next to the Monastiraki flea market
where he claimed to sell antiques. She'd wanted to take him by
surprise, demand an immediate answer.

She invited Andonis next door for an *ouzo* to discuss some
business. He fitted a navy fisherman's cap over his thinning grey
hair and shuffled toward the door. In the sunlight, his bloodshot
eyes and mottled skin affirmed his fondness for drink.

When she brought up the olive press, Andonis squinted suspi-
ciously. "My cousin Loukas sent you."

"I've never met Loukas," she countered, as if her feelings had
been hurt. "Did he try to buy the press from you?"

"He tried to steal it. He offered nothing."

"We could discuss an offer, but you'd have to separate out the
press from the land package."

"What package? Loukas said that?" he shouted. "It's a trick."

Alexis moved in fast. "Then trick him back. Sell me the press
without saying anything." Time to mention money. "The press
was valued at half a million drachmas when you inherited it ten
years ago."

He eyed her warily. "Half a million for the tax office, but it's
worth much more. I want five million drachmas."

The negotiation proceeded. Andonis held the line until Alexis
declared a final offer of two million drachma and an immediate
cash deposit which she slapped down on the table. He broke into
a beatific smile, fingered the money, counting out loud, scurried
over to his shop for copies of the deed.

When he returned, a bit unsteady on his feet, he signed the

sales agreement with a flourish. "*Kalo riziko*." Good rooting. The traditional greeting had sounded just right to Alexis.

Obviously, Loukas had been infuriated by the sale. His actions over the next six months proved it. She opened the notebook Georgia had brought. Time to get it all down.

She'd moved to Serros in a fierce January storm. Bundled up in an old gray raincoat and plaid scarf, her landlady, Sophia, met her at the ferry, brought her home to a meal of lentil soup laced with vinegar, and put her to bed under a heavy woolen blanket.

By the time Alexis woke from her nap, all signs of the storm had passed, leaving an intensely blue-black sky dotted with glittering constellations. She hung her jeans and workshirts in the cupboard and took a glass of home-made cherry brandy, a gift from *yiayia*, Sophia's mother, out to the porch. She'd reconnected with the Greece she loved—the awesome beauty, the vital human dimension. As she gazed at the star-bright gulf, she felt comfortable with her solitude. Perhaps for the first time in her life.

That had been her last moment of true peace. The next morning, she'd headed over to the construction yard. It looked like a tornado had swept through—cement sacks had spilled open, sand and lime were strewn about, rivulets of water crisscrossed the muddy ground. Her order of wood and roof tiles was piled next to the fence. The Pirate, as the owner was locally known, must have thought he wasn't going to get paid. Alexis found him in his office, shouting into the phone, one cigarette in his hand, another behind his ear.

Finally, he slammed down the receiver. "What do you want?"

"Mr. Elias, you promised weeks ago to deliver my order to the *liotrivi*."

"I'm too busy."

"Perhaps not today. I see you need to clean up after the storm, but when?"

"I don't know." He rifled through the clutter on his desk.

"I'm ready to start. If you don't deliver, who will?"

"You must find a truck." He turned away. That was all Alexis was going to get from him.

She slammed the office door. The bearded worker in the yard watched her.

She marched over. "Do you know what's going on here?"

He took off his wool cap, ran his fingers through his thick blond hair. Alexis was struck by his fair coloring and light blue eyes, unusual features in Greece.

"A man came here," he said, "short, very fat, from Athens. He asked the boss not to send out your order."

"I see." She hoped the worker wouldn't get in trouble for giving away the Pirate's game. "What's your name?"

"Theodoros."

"Are you from here?"

He laughed softly. "A village not very different from Serros."

Alexis sought out Nassos, handsome, gray-haired cafe-owner and source of all Serros gossip. He identified the fat man as her neighbor, Loukas Koutsos. Related to half the town, Loukas had convinced the Serrians to deny her transportation. Evidently, Loukas had bragged he'd force the American to buy *his* land, at a handsome price.

The pattern was established that day—point, counterpoint; Koutsos attack, Davidov defense. Furious, Alexis decided to transport the materials herself. The following morning, the Pirate watched with his mouth open as Alexis loaded her van with tiles. When she got to the lumber, Theodoros came over to help lift it onto the roof rack. The Pirate yelled at him. The worker swore back under his breath.

Exhausted, Alexis barely completed three trips that day. She tried to enlist the help of her roofer, Lefteris, but his wife said he was in Athens, out of contact. An unlikely story. Greeks were always within reach of a phone.

Loukas' second gambit—queering it with her workers. Potentially catastrophic. Workmen from Athens would double her labor costs.

Alexis grinned to herself, put down her pen. She couldn't write this part of the story—it would make the police too suspicious. But there was no harm in remembering.

The next day, Theodoros again helped her. Alexis wondered about this worker who was willing to stand up to his boss. He asked for a ride to Pygi when they had the van fully loaded. She was happy to oblige.

After they'd traveled a few minutes, Theodoros cleared his throat. "I build houses—wood and stone work—everything but plumbing and electricity." He looked steadily out the window. "I could work for you at the *liotrivi*. I've fixed many stone houses in Albania."

Instantly, the picture came into focus. "You're Albanian."

"I'm from Epirus, a Greek whose family moved years ago to southern Albania."

"Do you have a work permit?"

He pulled out a battered wallet. "It's good for another six months."

"What about your boss? Will he let you work for me?"

"I'll leave. He doesn't pay much."

"I can pay only the basic wage."

"That's more than I'm making now."

She shouldn't have been surprised. "Where would you live?"

"In the *liotrivi*. I can get more done if I live there."

"There's no heat; the roof has holes in it."

"I've seen it. The north end is dry."

Alexis hadn't planned on a full-time workman, but it appeared that was all she'd get. The locals would probably frown on an Albanian staying in the press. He'd have to keep a low profile. Still, the idea of working with him was appealing. "Theodoros, I'll let you know tomorrow."

"It's easier to call me Theo."

"Theo, then." She was approaching the back road to the olive press. "Can you help me unload? After, I'll bring you around to Pygi."

"No need. I'll come back to the harbor with you."

So he'd hitched a ride to ask for work. She liked his style—low-key but direct. She figured they'd get along just fine.

Her stomach rumbled. Where was the matron? Alexis hobbled to the door, called out for her morning coffee, then gaped in wonder. The matron appeared with a tray of fresh croissants, butter, jam, real orange juice, filter coffee. Georgia had arranged for breakfast.

Alexis dug into the food.

She and Theo *had* gotten along—from the start. The next morning, he'd pulled up to Sophia's in a large truck he'd obtained from the Pirate who, furious, wanted Theo and her order out of his sight.

Sophia had clucked her teeth in dismay. "Alexi, the village is going to talk. A handsome man and a beautiful woman. They'll suspect you of everything. Please be careful."

She thought she had been. Theo had been her workman. That was all. Yes, they'd become friends; yes, he'd stayed in her house, but only until she'd moved in. They'd spent many hours alone together, but they'd done absolutely nothing to bring a suspicion of conspiracy down on their heads.

She felt a new spasm shoot through her. She wasn't yet out of the woods. She pushed herself up from the table, leaned against the wall. She needed to lie down but even with the extra pillow, the sagging cot would make things worse. She edged her way to the door to call the matron.

The matron trudged up. "What is it?"

"I can't lie on that bed. I need to put the mattress on the floor. I'm sure my aunt will appreciate your help."

The matron yanked the mattress off the cot. "Anything else?"

"Can you help me down?"

Alexis gripped the chair in one hand and the matron's arm in the other. She sank to her knees. "Please push the mattress over here."

She kneeled forward, stretched out her arms, and lowered herself. "Whew. Much better. Thanks."

She lay on her back, stared at the peeling paint. Enough pleasant memories. Time to face the fears she'd ignored since yesterday.

Theo had been seen at the harbor. Had the police questioned him, detained him? She wondered if her lawyers would tell her. She had to know, protect this man who'd helped her from the beginning.

Stop it, she told herself. Maria and Nikos had always been straight with her. Soon, it would all be moot. The autopsy report would be released, her petition reviewed, and she'd be free.

The words sounded hollow. What was keeping her from believing them—anxiety or a strong dose of realism?

CHAPTER 4

At ten a.m., a new matron picked up the breakfast tray. She muttered, "In five minutes, you shower."

Alexis eagerly collected the shampoo, soap, and towels Georgia had brought. A half hour passed with no sign of the matron. The woman was a pig, even looked like one—round, pink, coarse hair—not unlike Loukas. In fact, a lot like Loukas. Alexis called out through the door. No response. She took up her pen, resumed writing to stave off her gathering fury. Better to direct it at Loukas where it belonged.

Round two. At the end of January, she'd gone to Athens to reason with Loukas. Although she had Theo, she needed a local electrician and plumber. She had to end the blackball.

She'd found his accounting office in a run-down building off the central market. A young male assistant in thick glasses motioned her in. Two men were shouting in the next room. Familiar profanities the only words discernible.

The assistant hurried into the inner sanctum. Hushed conversation. Then the office door flew open to reveal Loukas, his pea-green jacket stretching over his enormous paunch, his round face flushed, black bristles encircling a bald pate. He introduced his partner, Ioannidis, as gaunt as Loukas was rotund, pasty complexion, cold gray eyes that belied the pseudo-smile on his face.

Loukas barked at the assistant to bring coffee as he tugged Alexis toward a metal chair. He fixed his porcine gaze on her. "How are you enjoying Serros?"

"Very much." Although eager to get down to business, she feigned cordiality as custom required.

"A lovely island, still unspoiled. I hope all the new residents are fine people like yourself. Do you mind if I smoke? I know you Americ—"

"No, that's fine. Mr. Koutsos, I believe you know what I came about."

"You wish to buy my olive orchard." He spoke with utter conviction.

"I wish I could, but I can't."

Ioannidis, leaning against the wall, intervened. "There is no wish that can't be achieved between reasonable people."

Loukas drew a balled-up handkerchief from his pocket to wipe the sweat from his brow. "In any event, I have dropped my price. Ten million drachma—a great bargain for over one hundred producing olive trees."

"But I'm not in the oil production business. I'm a teacher. Even if your land were one-tenth the price, I simply couldn't afford it."

Loukas shrugged, clasped his hands across his mid-section. "Then, I suppose we have nothing to discuss except—"

Ioannidis finished his sentence. "Except the road."

"What road?"

Ioannidis smirked. "The road you use to deliver your materials that runs through Mr. Koutsos' land. You're using it illegally. As we speak, Mr. Koutsos' cousin and fellow land-owner, Panayiotis Koutsos, is installing a lock on the gate." He sipped his coffee. "You might think further about purchasing the olive orchard."

Alexis glowered. "The seller, Andonis Koutsos, also a cousin, informed me there has always been public access. This is pure harassment, but it won't work." As she stalked out, she heard them sniggering.

Ioannidis' image before her, Alexis sat deep in thought. She was sure he'd orchestrated Loukas' attacks on her. Nikos had said he'd disappeared. For good reason. Loukas' murder, the depositing of his corpse in the orchard, bore his trademark. The police had to find him.

After the confrontation in Loukas' office, Alexis had dashed back to Serros, headed straight for the *liotrivi*. The iron gate across the road was locked; a huge, shiny padlock taunted her like a personal insult. She marched in a fury up the rocky path to her house.

Theo was cutting new beams and crossbars for the roof. He'd installed himself in the dry end of the main room—bedroll, small gas stove, kerosene lamp, table, and chair. With wood shavings in his hair, he appeared a contented man.

He listened to Alexis' report, stroked his beard. "We'll improve the mountain path, make it wide and smooth enough for your van. I'll need a week."

"That's impossible."

"Not if I have help. I can get three Albanian boys I know on Aegina."

"Are they legal?"

Theo shrugged. "Everyone uses them. You'll have to pay transportation, food, basic wage. It will probably cost a hundred thousand drachma. Can you afford that?"

Alexis didn't hesitate. "I'll find the money. Theo, you live up to your name—you're a gift from God." She laughed, said in English, "My own personal road gang."

Just then, the matron shoved open the window and said, "Phone. Your lawyer."

Maria was on the line. "Alexi, let me give you the bad news first. We still don't have the autopsy report. They won't say when they'll release it."

Alexis swallowed hard. "What does that mean?"

"They found something they didn't expect."

"Something to identify the murderer?"

"Could be. I just don't know. There *is* a positive development, however."

"What?"

"Loukas' wife, Nitsa, and his cousin, Panayiotis, have initiated a suit against Ioannidis, who apparently was robbing the business of large sums of money. The police discovered Ioannidis flew to Cyprus Monday morning."

Alexis felt a rush of excitement. "Are they bringing him back?"

"As soon as they find him."

"It's obvious, Maria. He's on the run."

"We can't be sure. Right now, all we can do is wait."

The thought of more waiting triggered anger. Why wasn't Maria working this angle to get her out? Maybe Alexis did need someone with pull, someone like Roussakis. "Wait how long?"

"At most, another forty-eight hours."

"Forty-eight hours? That makes five days in this hole."

"I don't think it will be that long. What can we do to help you bear it?"

Alexis sighed. "Nothing. Just do what you need to do, but fast, please."

"We will, Alexi. I'll call again this afternoon."

Alexis dragged back to the cell. How could she take another forty-eight hours? She closed her eyes. Think of a time when you were strong, she whispered to herself, when you took them on and won. The end of round two.

Theo's workers had arrived on a wild day; the ferry, buffeted by fierce winds, docked with difficulty. The young Albanians, in jeans and thin windbreakers, ran down the pier to the van. She and Theo had to spirit them away before the townspeople guessed what was up.

The *liotrivi* was well-stocked with food and blankets. Alexis had borrowed tools from Sophia, but they had only two picks and two shovels. Theo said they'd make do; Albanians often worked only with their hands. He'd insisted Alexis stay in town, not draw attention to the activity at the press. He'd phoned the fourth morning to say the road would be done by evening if she wanted to inspect it.

The treacherous path had been widened to two meters, the protruding rocks, removed and reset, the earthen sections, smoothed out with small stones and sand. Alexis glowed with victory as the van made it up easily.

"The boys never stopped working," Theo said. "That's why we're done a day early."

"I'll still pay them what I promised."

"I knew you'd say that." He seemed to trust her as much as she'd come to trust him.

Inside, the young men sat around a plastic sheet on the floor, consuming huge portions of spaghetti and jabbering in Albanian.

Theo laughed. "They're commenting, favorably and not so favorably, on my cooking. After dinner, they'll leave, sleep in the hills."

"Why? It's cold."

"It's safer. I heard murmuring in Pygi."

Alexis passed around the *retsina* she'd brought. "I'd like to know about the area they come from."

Theo translated. The three boys remained silent.

Finally, a towhead with pink cheeks said, "Our village is high, just below the snow line. We have fresh running water all year long, but no indoor bathrooms."

The others snickered, but the boy ignored them. "We have electricity," he said, as if describing a miracle.

"What work did you do?" Alexis asked.

"There is no work," a brown-haired boy with a long nose declared. "That's why we're here. Speaking of outdoor plumbing."

He got up to go outside. Laughing, the others joined him. Suddenly, the front door banged open. The blond croaked something in Albanian.

Theo sprang up, grabbed their jackets. "The money, Alexi."

She scrambled for her purse, handed him an envelope. As he thrust the jackets and money at the boys, he hissed instructions. In an instant, they were gone.

"Someone's coming up the path," Theo said. "Go to the kitchen."

From the back, she detected sounds of a scuffle outside. Theo rushed in, grabbed his wallet, strode out.

A man shouted, "Don't forget, you break the law, your papers mean nothing."

Theo stepped back in, massaging his arm.

Her stomach turning over, Alexis approached him. "What happened?"

"Villagers. They wanted me to admit I had illegal workers here. I told them some kids came by looking for work. I fed them and sent them on their way. Of course, they didn't believe me." He looked smug. "The road's too much work for one man, even me."

"What will happen if they catch the boys?"

"They'll beat them, rob them, hand them to the police to send back."

"What a terrible end to the week."

"Alexi, you have your road. A fishing boat will pick the boys up on the other side of the island. Just to be safe, I'll leave for a few days."

"Where will you go?"

"Albania."

She shuddered. "What if they won't let you back?"

"I know how to get back. We all do."

Theo *had* come back, Alexis mused. He'd kept his promise, all his promises.

And the promised shower? She'd been waiting two hours. Through the window, she yelled in frustration.

The matron finally appeared. "No shower now." She grunted. "You have a meeting."

"What meeting?"

"Police," she said with a sneer.

Alexis wanted to strangle her. "I won't talk to anyone without my lawyers."

"Don't worry. They're here too."

*   *   *

"Sit down, Alexi." Nikos pulled out a chair at the small table where Maria perched like a sparrow, her red nails tapping, a peeved look on her face.

"How's your back?" he asked.

"Better, thank you."

"Good. Let's talk before the detectives start the interrogation." The three leaned in close.

"Alexi, they found a gun," Maria murmured, "at the *liotrivi*."

Alexis' eyes shot from one lawyer to the other. "You won't believe this. I forgot about the gun."

"Forgot?" they repeated, almost simultaneously.

It sounded crazy to her own ears, but it was true. "Theo gave it to me on his last day in Serros. I didn't want it, but he insisted."

"Why?" Nikos asked sternly.

"To scare people off." She took a deep breath. "This was just after the Easter incident."

"What did you do with the gun?"

"I put it back in Theo's hiding place. On a ledge in the stone wall behind his bed. Now, behind the sofa. It's been there ever since."

"Can you think of any way the gun might be linked to Loukas' murder?"

"Only if someone found it and used it. That couldn't be. I slept at the press every night from the time Theo left until the fire."

"Could someone have taken it during the day when you were out?" Maria said.

"Anyway, there were no bullets," Alexis said, feeling dazed. "If Loukas was shot, it couldn't have been with that gun."

Nikos grimaced. "As far as you know."

"I'm sure."

"Okay, Alexi. Tell the detectives the truth. They probably know from ballistics tests the gun wasn't fired recently, but they're going to use it as an excuse to hold you, link you to Theo." He looked worried. "Downplay your connection with Theo. He gave you the gun as a friendly gesture, because you were a woman alone."

"Don't forget you haven't seen him at all since then," Maria muttered.

Nikos waved the two detectives over. "You can start." He stood directly across from Alexis, ready to prompt her.

The younger detective looked like a weightlifter—beefy neck, wide face with a brown crewcut, bulging build. He placed a cassette recorder on the table. "Miss Davidov, we're recording this interrogation. It can be entered as evidence in a court of law. You may consult your lawyers before you answer. Is that clear?"

Alexis, discomfort mounting, nodded.

"Please answer verbally. Is that clear?"

"Yes."

"Okay. While searching your home in Serros, we found a gun hidden in the living room wall. Whose gun is it?"

"Mine."

"How long have you had that gun?"

"About two months."

"Where'd you get it?"

"It was given to me by my stonemason."

"Name?"

"Theodoros Argiros."

"Where does he reside?"

"In Nemea."

"Why did he leave Serros?"

"He finished the job."

"But he returns to Serros?"

The first trap. "Not that I know of."

"You haven't heard from him since he stopped working for you?"

"No."

The detective seemed stymied, then said, "When did he leave Serros?"

She gazed at the ceiling as if trying to remember. "At the end of April."

"You haven't seen or talked to him since?"

"No."

The second detective, pushing sixty, sallow skin, greasy hair combed over his bald spot, broke in. "Why did Argiros give you a gun?"

"For protection. He knew I'd be living alone in a fairly remote place."

"Women don't use guns to protect themselves."

"Maybe not in Greece. They do in America." She sounded like a member of the NRA. "In any case, it was only to scare people away."

Nikos coughed, shot her a warning look. She'd tumbled right into the second trap.

"Your neighbors?"

"Certainly not. I didn't plan to use the gun. I took it, hid it away, and forgot about it."

"You forgot about it?" The detective raised his voice to bully her.

It had the opposite effect. She sat straighter. "Obviously, or I would have mentioned it to the police."

"Miss Davidov, you got this gun only two months ago."

"I forgot about it the same day I got it. Out of sight, out of mind."

Alexis saw a hint of a smile cross Maria's face. She took heart.

"Where are the bullets, Miss Davidov?"

"There are no bullets. As I told you, the gun wasn't for shooting."

"Then what use did it have?"

To complicate my life, Alexis thought. "Obviously, none."

Nikos stepped over to Alexis. "My client has told you all she can about the gun."

The younger detective waved him back. "I'm not done. Miss Davidov, you know Argiros is Albanian."

"Greek Albanian."

"He's an immigrant."

"A legal immigrant."

"Even legal immigrants are prohibited from possessing guns in Greece."

"That must be why he gave it to me."

"*You* are also in violation of the law."

"I didn't know."

Maria came over, put her hand on Alexis' shoulder. "It's a minor violation, Detective, possession of an unarmed weapon. Unless you can demonstrate the gun's been used by my client."

The older detective switched off the machine, smoothed a strand of hair over his head. "We'll see what the Albanian has to say."

He'd stepped on Alexis' tripwire.

"For God's sake," she cried. "Why aren't you looking for the real murderer?"

"Don't worry. We've cast our net widely." The younger detective stood, a smirk on his face. "See you at the hearing. Maybe Miss Davidov's memory will improve by then."

After they left, Maria and Nikos again took their seats at the table.

"Good job, Alexi," Maria murmured.

Alexis felt drained. "What if Theo—"

"Alexi, we've warned Theo," Nikos said. "The most they can get him for is a minor gun violation."

"Then what's this all about?"

"It's a smokescreen to keep you here. They're still trying to prove Theo was in Serros during the fire. The testimony they have is not enough to charge either of you with murder."

Maria frowned. "We'll know more from the autopsy report this afternoon. No one's saying whether or not Loukas was shot. We'll call you as soon as we have it, but we won't get you out of here today."

Another day inside. "What about Ioannidis?"

"They're still looking or him."

Alexis nodded, not trusting herself to speak.

CHAPTER 5

Back in her cell, Alexis found herself sweating. Her pulse thumped like an electric bass. What if Loukas *had* been shot? What if Ioannidis had somehow gotten hold of her gun?

She thought again about Roussakis, weighed the option. By now, he'd have detectives out looking for Ioannidis. Still, Maria and Nikos were working not only on her behalf, but also Theo's. Would a lawyer like Roussakis help her cover for Theo? Not likely. He might get her out of jail, but he'd sacrifice Theo in the process.

She lay down again, thought about the detectives' obsession with Theo. Her stonemason. In the beginning, he'd been just that. Only in Athens had he become a person with a past.

When, after fixing the path, Theo left for Albania, Alexis had set out for Athens. She wanted to shop and catch up with Vaso. The two women had formed a strong bond from the day Alexis arrived at Lincoln American School. A New York University graduate, Vaso had sought her out. Partly Americanized, Vaso understood, and often shared, Alexis' views. For her part, Alexis treasured having a Greek friend who could *and would* frankly interpret Greece for her.

Vaso hugged Alexis at the front door. "A message. Theodoros Argiros phoned. He's with friends in the Peristeri area. Is he the Albanian?"

Alexis' eyes, the color of tourmaline, sparkled like gems. "Yes."

"You were worrying he wouldn't return."

"Now I'm worrying about keeping him in Athens until my plumber finishes. Theo will want to go right back to Serros, even though *he* convinced *me* he should stay out of sight of other work-men. I'll have to play tour guide."

"I'd like to meet this character. How about I cook you both dinner tomorrow? I'll invite Cliff for male company."

This was the Americanized Vaso, Alexis thought. A typical Greek wouldn't offer dinner at home for a workman.

"Wonderful. I'll pick up wine and dessert."

*   *   *

The next morning, a bitterly cold wind whipped the few tourists huddling at the Acropolis ticket office. Alexis had dressed in lay-ers—leggings under jeans, a turtleneck and pullover under one of Vaso's bulky ski sweaters. When she spotted Theo in a thin wind-breaker, her heart went out to him. "Theo, you made it back."

"Not hard." He rubbed his fingers together to signify a bribe. "How are you?"

"Very cold. Ready for the history lesson?"

They climbed to the sanctuary on the rock. Alexis concen-trated on details she thought would interest Theo, was impressed by his questions.

What if it had all ended with the Acropolis? She and Theo would have returned to Serros, employer and workman, perhaps more like co-workers, but not a hint of anything more.

But it hadn't.

Alexis pushed back her chair, caught sight of a many-legged creature crawling under the bathroom door into the cell. She was filled with disgust. She had nothing to kill it with except a book. She couldn't. With relief, she watched the centipede stop, then turn around, probably to escape back down the bathroom drain.

She had to escape this place, at least in her mind. She attacked her long hair with her brush, propelled herself back to that freez-ing day in Athens.

When Alexis had proposed lunch at The Vines, a picturesque

taverna in Plaka owned by friends, Theo winced. "Alexi, I left all my money in Albania for my parents and daughter."

She was stunned. She'd never stopped to ask Theo about family, had assumed he was unmarried. "Your daughter?"

"I have an eight year old. She lives with my parents."

"Your wife, too?"

"My daughter's mother . . . It's a long story. You want me to tell you?"

"At lunch. Don't worry about paying. Costas won't take money from me."

She led Theo through the narrow streets, up a short stairway to a *taverna* doorway framed by arching branches of grape vines. Costas threw his arms around Alexis. He seated them next to the fireplace, went to the kitchen, and came back with his wife and a carafe of tawny home-made wine.

"How is Tassos doing?" Alexis asked when free from Eleni's embrace.

Costas puffed up. "He graduates from Columbia in June. All because of you."

"No, Costa *mou*, Tassos is very clever."

His eyes twinkled. "Like his father. Now, your news."

Alexis introduced Theo, described the restoration. Costas interrupted every few moments with *bravo*, ordered his wife to the kitchen to prepare a feast—huge servings of lamb fricassee and beet salad.

Theo ate ravenously.

Costas clapped him on the back. "Today, you are my best customer. I will bring quinces for dessert."

Theo took one last swipe of his plate with a piece of bread. "Shall I tell you about my daughter now?"

Alexis nodded.

"Actually, Olga is the middle of the tale. I'll start when I went off to Tirana University. The regime was becoming more and more authoritarian. We couldn't have contact with the outside world, read foreign newspapers or literature, be religious, be Greek. I spoke out only twice. A small matter—the right to do research without government control."

"What happened?"

"My parents lost their teaching jobs. My brother was arrested for smuggling—a lie. I was jailed and tortured. My parents paid a huge bribe, and I was secretly released. I had to go underground."

Alexis was riveted. "How long?"

"About a year. I changed houses every night. You can see why sleeping in the *liotrivi* is a luxury. A girl helped me hide, from the north, not Greek." Theo stared into his wine glass, sadness in his eyes. "She pleaded with me to go north with her, then announced she was pregnant."

The age-old impasse, Alexis thought.

"I believed it was a trick to keep me. I went back to the university. She went home. When I next saw her, I had a baby daughter. I thought maybe she was someone else's, but Olga looks just like me. I fell in love with my daughter. Her mother insisted we get married. I agreed to live with them, support them, but I wouldn't marry her."

"A kind of solution, I guess."

"Not in Albania. The girl appealed to her family to save her from dishonor. She's from the region of blood feuds and revenge." He looked away. "I ran, but with my daughter."

"God, what a story."

"Olga's mother never came for her. My parents are raising Olga until I can bring them all to Greece."

Even then, even after hearing Theo's story, Alexis mused, they might have gone on as before—friendly, but not close. Vaso's dinner party had been the clincher.

When Alexis returned that afternoon, loaded with packages, Vaso was setting the dining table. "Your Albanian's coming?"

"Yes. He's not *my* Albanian. You make him sound like an indentured servant."

"Maybe you're a little sensitive. Is he any different from *your* Filipinessa, the cleaning girl you had?"

"I never said *my* Filipinessa. In any case, he's a university graduate who happens to be a skilled workman."

"Sorry. Sometimes we Greeks get a little categorical about foreigners. Would you get the door?"

Cliff waved a bottle of Scotch, put his arm around Alexis. "The Social Studies Program has been peaceful—and dull—since you left us."

They gossiped, but Alexis was only half-there. When the bell rang again, she sprang up. Theo held daisies for Vaso in one hand, a package wrapped in brown paper in the other. "From my village. You like old things."

Theo had brought her an intricately embroidered vest, vivid flowers against a royal blue velvet background. "It's lovely."

As Theo held Alexis' gaze, Vaso broke in. "What would you like to drink?"

The teachers resumed their conversation in Greek.

After a moment, Theo said in English, "I'd like you to speak English. My ear doesn't get much practice."

Alexis stared, shocked.

"I've been studying," he explained. "I was going to tell you when I improved."

"You are full of surprises."

Cliff grilled Theo about conditions in Albania. Theo's answers were filled with humor, his English occasionally the butt of a friendly joke. After the meal, Cliff drained his wine glass, hugged his colleagues, and offered Theo a ride to the bus stop.

Vaso immediately pounced. "You're in trouble, my dear. Theo's in love with you."

"Vaso, he's a very nice man who has helped me a lot . . . "

"You're wrong, Alexi, and you're being naive. You *cannot* have an affair with an Albanian."

"It's not an affair. If anything, it's the beginning of a friendship."

"Alexi *mou*, you are always pushing boundaries. You can't even have a friendship with an Albanian without jeopardizing all you've got in Greece."

"Why the hell not?"

"He's a good-looking man and you're a stunning woman. In Greece, that's perceived as a sexual connection. And, however nice he is, he's from a backward country. How would he ever fit into your world?"

"He fit in tonight, didn't he?"

"Alexi, you were with two close friends—another American and a Greek educated in America—who made him fit. Just picture Theo at one of Diana's parties."

"That's absurd. No, wait. I'm mouthing your biases. Why wouldn't he survive a fancy dinner party?"

"Did you see the way he ate?"

"For heaven's sake. Table manners are the surface."

"Here, the surface is read like a computer print-out. What about his interests, emotional development?"

"He's more emotionally developed than many of my Greek friends."

Vaso, brow furrowed, wordlessly folded the tablecloth.

"I don't mean you, Vaso. I was thinking of Petros. Look, I'm only defending Theo because I felt you attacked him. As soon as I finish the *liotrivi*, he'll be out of my life."

Theo hadn't disappeared from her life. If not for the fire, he might have. Odd, to be grateful for the fire.

The key turned in the cell door. Her shower, finally. She picked up her bath things.

A straw basket filled with packages was kicked into the cell. The door closed, the lock clicked.

Alexis stalked to the window and yelled, "What about the shower?"

"Not now."

"Damn it. I've been waiting all morning."

"Later."

"What is this basket?"

"It was left for you."

"By whom?"

"Some lady in red sneakers."

Sophia's trademark. With her traditional widow's black, she wore her daughter's red sneakers as a way of keeping Eleftheria, now in Athens, close.

Alexis dragged the basket over to her chair, dug inside. Sophia's idea of sustenance—a jar of olives, thyme honey, a wheel of *kasseri* cheese, biscuits, figs and peaches. A note was stuffed in the bag of peaches.

> Alexi *mou*: They won't let me in. This is from me and Popi. I had to take the *retsina* out—not allowed. We all miss you terribly. Georgia says you will be back soon. Serros is recovering from the fire. Much of the forest burned, but only one house. Popi has the cats. They're fine. Come home soon to your island and your Sophia.

Alexis could barely read through her tears. In the last few days, she'd lost her bearings. She'd desperately needed a reminder of what this struggle was all about.

A basket of food and love. She felt as if a gentle hand had reached out, pulled her back from the edge of a deep abyss, and led her home.

CHAPTER 6

Late Tuesday afternoon, another new matron, middle-aged, with a tight gray permanent wave and blue eyes, knocked, then gently opened the door of Alexis' cell. "Your lawyers are back to see you, dear. Will you come now?"

Alexis wanted to embrace the woman who'd not only spoken nicely, but also brought good news. "Thank you. Let's go."

Nikos sat pensively at the table, Maria paced on her high heels behind him. Hardly a scene of jubilation.

"Am I getting out?" Alexis asked without even greeting them.

"They scheduled the hearing for noon tomorrow," Nikos said softly.

"At last." She hesitated. "You two seem down."

Nikos rubbed his hands together. "Ioannidis is back from Cyprus. He has a solid alibi for last Saturday. A family wedding in Megara from Friday evening until Sunday."

"No," Alexis cried. "He's lying."

"There are dozens of witnesses, Alexi."

"Then he planned the murder. Someone else executed it."

"He's still a suspect, but it will take a lot more investigation. Still, we don't think they'll hold you."

She went cold. "You don't *think* they'll hold me? You two need to tell me what's going on."

Maria frowned. "A piece of the puzzle is still missing. The autopsy report. They're not giving it to us until tomorrow at nine."

Alexis swayed on her feet.

Nikos quickly helped her to a chair. "It appears they timed the hearing to give us little opportunity to review the report."

"And if there's something incriminating?"

"We ask for more time. Right now, we've got to prepare you for the hearing. Are you okay?"

She nodded weakly.

Maria stood before her, gestured with both arms. "Here's the Piraeus courtroom, bare walls, poorly illuminated, hard wooden benches. I'm one of three judges sitting on high, black robe, stern face. The prosecutor's down below, on the right. Expect Loukas' grieving widow, Nitsa, to be in the gallery. Also a swarm of curious relatives."

Nikos stood across from Maria. "We'll be on the left side. Georgia will be directly behind us to translate anything too technical for you."

Alexis exhaled deeply, relieved Georgia would be there.

"You'll have to testify, Alexi, about how you found the body. You may have to go into your relationship with Loukas. You speak only about how Loukas harassed you. Not a word about how you got him back."

He came over to her, spoke in a hush. "The one thing you must remember is *only* Yiannis was there the night of the fire. *He* cut all the trees. When you went out to survey the next morning, you were with Yiannis. We've obtained a statement from Popi's husband, Thanos, swearing you told him a male friend, Yiannis, was coming to help. That's our best evidence."

The matron approached the table. "The showers shut down in twenty minutes," she murmured apologetically.

"Oh God. I must have a shower," Alexis said. "Will I see you again before the hearing?"

"Only if necessary. Are you okay with that?"

"I guess."

"Go have a long shower," Maria said. "Tomorrow won't be as amusing as our last court session, but we'll get you out of here and home."

*   *   *

Glorying in the stream of lukewarm water, Alexis considered Maria's words. *Not as amusing as our last court session.* Not exactly amusing, but it had had its moments.

When Alexis and Theo had returned to Serros from Athens, their lives entered into a delightful routine. Alexis left for the olive press each morning after an early breakfast with Sophia. While Theo cut and fit wood for the doors, window frames, and shutters, Alexis stained the wood a dark walnut, applied coats of varnish to make it gleam.

They shared bread, cheese, and apples at break time. Alexis usually brought a newspaper for Theo who was fascinated by world news. They steered away from personal topics. Any hint of a personal relationship would set the Serrians off on a binge of gossip and hurt them both. Alexis knew Vaso hadn't been totally off base; she kept a polite if friendly distance.

Suddenly the shower shut off. Alexis toweled dry, called the matron to take her back to the cell. Feeling clean made such a difference. Re-energized, she decided to finish the notes she'd started—if just for posterity.

Round three—Loukas' next move. While she'd been in Athens, he'd come to Serros, stuck a contraption of sheet metal on spikes in the ground in front of her kitchen window. No air, no light.

Alexis' plumber, Michalis, had reportedly tried to stop him, but, strictly speaking, Loukas hadn't encroached upon her property. Alexis was forced to sue, something she'd been strenuously avoiding.

In early March, Maria got the lawsuit onto that month's court calendar. "We must prove your kitchen was once a place of human habitation. Then we can assert you're restoring an existing window."

"That's all true. It was a storeroom, but during the harvest, the workers stayed there to press the olives."

"Your job, Alexi, is to get sworn statements to that effect."

"No problem."

"Don't be so sure. Most Greeks won't get involved in court

cases. I doubt Serrians are any different."

Alexis consulted Sophia who was dusting her china birds in the parlor.

Sophia grimaced. "No one will testify. Not from Pygi. They haven't forgotten the Albanian kids."

Alexis threw up her hands. "What am I going to do?"

"Get *pseudomartyres*."

"False witnesses?"

"You pay people to make statements or testify."

Sophia assured her it was done all the time. The Koutsos cousins would come to court with each and every body they could find.

"In America, that's against the law," Alexis said indignantly.

"Here, too, if you prove it."

"I'd rather lose the case."

Sophia turned back to dusting. "Then, you probably will."

No one in Pygi, not even Popi, had been willing to make a statement. Alexis debated buying witnesses. She'd adapted to so many other Greek customs, why not this one? Still, every time she considered it, she backed away.

She'd had such a clear idea of what was ethical then, knew her pride in the olive press would be lost if she used false witnesses. Now, without any hesitation, she was lying about Theo. What was the difference?

Alexis paced along the wall. There was a difference. In Serros, she would have been lying for her own selfish purpose; here, it was to protect an innocent man. That was partly it, but there was something more. Then, she still believed justice would prevail.

Michalis, her plumber, had come to the rescue. Summoned to the *cafeneion*, Alexis found him lounging at a table, two glasses and a small, half-empty bottle of *ouzo* in front of him. He noisily dragged out a chair for Alexis. "How are things at the *liotrivi*?"

"In another week, I'll be ready for you to install the fixtures."

He sized her up. "Before that, you need me to fight Koutsos."

She gaped. "You've heard. I need a statement saying the kitchen was a place where workers cooked and slept at night."

"I know that for a fact. I worked there as a young boy. But I won't give you a statement." He roared with laughter. "What a face on you. Listen, girl, I'm coming to court. To confront those bastards in person."

An ally. At last. Would he be too vindictive?

"Michali, thank you. I'll talk to the lawyers about your appearing as a witness."

He ignored her, downed the rest of the *ouzo* in one swallow.

*   *   *

A gentle knock sounded on the cell door—the matron with dinner.

Alexis pushed the tray aside. "Thank you, but I can't face any more fried food. I have some cheese and olives."

"You must eat for strength. Happily, you'll be leaving here tomorrow."

"You think so?"

"Of course. Anyone can see you're not a murderer."

"I appreciate your kindness. You're very different from the other matrons."

"I don't like this job, but I need the money. Another couple of months and I'll quit."

"You must, or you'll become like the rest of them. Could I ask a favor?"

"Yes."

"I'd like to call my friend, Vaso, and have her drop off clean clothes for my hearing."

The matron looked over her shoulder toward the door, then murmured, "You know you haven't had your visit today, only your lawyers."

"You'd let her come tonight?"

"You must keep the visit very short."

"Bless you."

Alexis made her call, then, exhausted, lay down to wait. She reviewed her lines for the hearing. Only Yiannis was there. *He* cut down the trees. *He* was with her when she discovered Loukas' body. The thought of testifying made her shiver. If she slipped up, Theo would pay.

The matron knocked softly, took away the dinner tray, came back with two cups of tea. "Would you like to chat a bit? It might calm your nerves."

"Thank you for understanding. Sit down, please. What is your name?"

"Katerina." The matron pulled out the plastic chair and faced Alexis who was curled up on the cot. "A Greek court must be hard for a foreigner."

"I've been to court before."

Alexis stopped short. What if Katerina were a plant from the police? Or was that paranoid? She reminded herself she had nothing to hide, as long as she didn't mention Theo. She wanted, needed to talk. "That case was different."

Very different. Loukas, straight from Athens, in a wool over-coat and fedora, looked out of place in Serros. He had his slimy partner with him and his wife, Nitsa, a young woman trying to look sophisticated, heavily made up, artificially blonde. She hung on the arm of a younger, taller man with thick black hair and eyebrows, chiseled features, and a black leather jacket, collar up—cousin Panayiotis. The *pseudomartyres* hopped around, scratching the ground like chickens.

The matron smiled. "Different? How?"

"All very informal," Alexis said. "The judge was in her thirties, red hair, wearing slacks. It was a petty issue. Loukas—the man who was murdered—blocked my kitchen window with sheet metal."

"Why?"

"To force me to buy his land."

Katerina inched to the edge of her chair. "What happened?"

"Loukas and his cousin tried to intimidate us. Their contingent, ten to twelve strong, occupied one side of the courtroom.

Our side was just me and my friend Sophia for support until my plumber, our star witness, burst into the courtroom, followed by hordes of relatives. The two groups of witnesses shouted obscenities at each other."

"How awful."

"It was actually comic. The judge threw the locals out. Then, Nikos, my lawyer, brought out photographs of the olive press taken before the restoration that clearly showed a window frame."

The matron giggled. "So that was that?"

"Almost. The judge came up to the house to examine the building. Loukas left for Athens, so his cousin, Panayiotis, came instead. The judge saw the old window frame which we'd preserved and declared it a window." Alexis laughed, the first time in days.

"Congratulations. It's not easy for foreigners to win these cases."

"It left hard feelings," Alexis said.

After the judge made her pronouncement, Panayiotis, who'd been smoking in a corner of the press, stepped forward, just short of Alexis, ground his cigarette on the dirt floor. "So," he said fiercely, "Greece is sold to the foreigners. Miss Davidov, you've taken our heritage. I hope you enjoy it."

"I purchased this place legally and I'm preserving it for posterity, something that should have happened long ago."

"I don't need to listen to your speeches." He strode outside, spat on the ground.

The judge shook her head. "We Greeks are not known for being good losers."

Nikos put his arm around Alexis. "That's all talk. He won't try anything else."

Alexis hadn't been at all sure. Loukas had proven a boor, but Panayiotis struck her as dangerous. She shuddered, remembering.

The matron seemed to sense her fear, tried to distract her. "Tell me about your friend who's coming tonight, Vaso. Has she seen your new home?"

Alexis didn't want to talk about Easter. Still, she wanted the matron to stay. "Over the Easter holiday, Vaso and another friend from school, Cliff, came to paint the kitchen and bathroom."

Vaso had actually come to persuade Alexis to return to teaching. As soon as she and Cliff had arrived and changed into work clothes, they took Alexis for coffee at the harbor.

Vaso was blunt. "Are you coming back or not? The rumors are flying."

Alexis was ready for them. "You both know I haven't been too happy at Lincoln lately. I still love the kids, and most of the faculty are fine. But the administration—especially Hudson—drives me nuts."

Cliff leaned forward, a serious look on his usually grinning features. "You're not alone, Alexi. You know that."

"I often *feel* I'm alone. Remember last year, when Hudson unilaterally cancelled my class on the Balkans because it was too controversial? You were the only social science teacher who spoke out."

"He's so disgusting," Vaso said. "He just terminated after school programs for the middle school so he can establish a money-making college prep course."

"It's going to keep happening unless we do something," Alexis countered. "Now, if I've learned anything from doing this house, it's that you've got to have allies."

Vaso looked wary. "So?"

"I'll come back in the fall and run for Faculty Council head *if* you two will be on my slate."

Vaso accused her of blackmail, Cliff worried about the time commitment. Alexis, knowing they'd agree, gave them the weekend to think about it.

The matron giggled. "Rich Americans repair their own houses. I've seen it on tv. We poor Greeks call a workman."

"Not all. My Aunt Georgia also joined the work party."

The matron's eyes stared in disbelief. "What did your aunt do?"

"My workman was finishing the floor planks. She hammered pegs into holes, said it was like kindergarten, but she worked hard."

"So, you had a workman."

Damn, why did she mention Theo? "Briefly," she lied.

The matron stood up to leave. "I must go. Your friend Vaso should be here soon."

"Thank you for talking with me."

After the matron left, Alexis again felt panicky. Had she talked too much?

CHAPTER 7

A half hour later, Vaso clutched Alexis in a tight bearhug. "You're so thin, *agapi mou*."

Alexis leaned against Vaso's ample frame. "It's a good place for a diet."

"Just what you don't need. I'd have come sooner, but I was sure you'd be out in a day." Vaso clasped Alexis by the shoulders, stared into her eyes. "Alexi, you seem so depressed. Are you ready for tomorrow?"

Alexis desperately wanted to confide her fears about the hearing—the mysterious autopsy report, having to lie before the court—but she couldn't take the risk. "Yes. You brought some clothes?"

"They'll hang on you. Here's a plain blue skirt and blouse to make you look innocent."

She swallowed hard. "I am innocent."

"Oh, Alexi, you know what I mean."

Vaso seemed different, awkward. Was it the setting or was she hiding something?

Alexis was becoming paranoid. She changed the subject. "What's new at summer school?"

"Everyone is really worried about you."

Her mouth dropped. "Everyone knows?"

Vaso shrugged helplessly. "This is Greece."

"God, that's awful." Alexis began to cry. "I didn't want anyone to know."

"Don't get upset, Alexi. It's just that so many people care about you."

She searched for a tissue in her jeans pocket, wiped her eyes.

"You have no idea what it's like to be here. You go over your life, try to figure out how you ended up in jail. You're anxious twenty-four hours a day, sick from the smell of your own body."

Vaso swept her friend up in her strong arms. "Please forgive me for not coming sooner."

"That's not my point. I'm trying to explain why I'm crying."

"*Pedi mou*, you don't need to explain. Tomorrow, it's over. I insist you come stay with me after the hearing. You can tell me every detail. But now you have to get hold of yourself."

"I will."

"Good. Get some rest. Go to bed thinking only of good things—your beautiful home, our wonderful Easter there."

Alexis flinched—she'd never told her friend about Easter Monday.

The matron came in, tugged Vaso gently by the arm. "I'm sorry. You must leave now. You're not really supposed to be here."

"I'm coming. Alexi, do you want me there tomorrow?"

"No, you're teaching. Georgia will be there for support."

"Good. Call me at school the minute it's over."

Alexis kissed her good-bye. "Please don't tell anyone about seeing me in jail."

The cell door closed. Alexis felt her heart pumping, pounding at her temples. She'd consciously pushed Easter out of her mind. It had come back only in dreams. Perhaps she'd been wrong to do that. Perhaps the key to her troubles lay there.

She dropped to the floor in the corner of her cell, as far as possible from the glare of the overhead light. *Think about our wonderful Easter.* Shivering, she let the memories in.

Brilliant sunshine had bathed the island as if blessing the day. All her dear friends from Serros, Athens, Nemea, had come to her Easter housewarming. Theo, Yiannis, and Pavlos, Sophia's future son-in-law, shared the traditional male job of turning the savory lamb on the spit. The rest of the meal, prepared by the three generations of women in Sophia's family—*yiayia*, Sophia, and Eleftheria—warmed in steel pans next to the fire. Exhausted by her hammering, Georgia refused to do anything but sit with a glass of wine.

Cliff sat beside her. "How many pegs was it, Georgia?"

"I stopped counting at ten thousand."

"Ten thousand?" Christina, Alexis' godchild, screeched.

Helen beckoned to her daughter. "I think Aunt Georgia's exaggerating. Let's go inside and see if we can figure out the real number."

Alexis, spotting her chance to speak alone with Yiannis, asked him to check out something on the path. When they were out of earshot of the others, she said, "You and Theo were deep in conversation last night. It's not my business, but I'm curious to know what's up."

"I was going to tell you, Alexi. When Theo leaves here, he's coming to work for me. I've bought more land. I need someone full time."

Alexis stopped in her tracks. "He's not going to spend the summer with his daughter?"

"He'll bring Olga to Nemea. She'll stay with Christina, help take care of the boys. If things work out over the summer, she'll move to Nemea, start school in the fall."

"Theo must be thrilled." Alexis felt a vague jealousy nag at her.

Yiannis drew on his pipe. "Alexi, Theo's worried about you. You didn't tell us the Koutsos cousins have appealed the case."

She kicked at a stone on the path. "Continuing harassment. Maria and Nikos are sure we'll win again, but I've got to pay for another round."

"You know we're ready to help."

"Thanks. I'm okay, just worn down by these jerks."

"That's exactly what they want. Alexi, you won't always be alone here. Theo plans to visit. Since the ferry from Nauplion to Serros runs on Friday and Sunday, we've arranged a schedule that would give him a long weekend off once a month. He wants to surprise you."

Alexis was confused. What did Theo expect to do on the weekends? Work? Keep her company? What would the folks in Pygi have to say?

"That's kind of Theo, but I'll be fine. I know you'll enjoy working with him, Yianni."

"He's a fine man, Alexi. I'm glad you found him."

She felt herself coloring at the possible double meaning. "He found me," she said as they turned back.

Within the hour, the cooks declared the lamb ready. Pans of roasted potatoes and onions, stuffed tomatoes and peppers, and a platter of rosemary-scented lamb were laid out on Theo's workbench. Borrowed chairs and small tables were scattered around the terrace.

Alexis hit a fork against a glass. "Before we eat, I'd like to make a toast, actually, many toasts." She held her glass in one hand, Christina in the other. "On this beautiful holiday, I thank you all for being here. Sophia, *yiayia*, Eleftheria and Pavlos, *evcharisto* for making me part of your family and giving me a home this winter. Helen and Yiannis, for your understanding of why I needed the *liotrivi*, and for the most wonderful godchild in the whole world."

Alexis bent down to kiss Christina, then said, "I've only one regret as far as Georgia's concerned—that she didn't come earlier. The way she works, I could have been finished months sooner."

"Wait 'til you get my bill," Georgia shouted.

Everyone roared.

"To Vaso and Cliff, thanks for not abandoning me when I left your lives for a few months."

Vaso gave Alexis a victory sign. "You win, Alexi. To the next Lincoln Faculty Council President."

Alexis faced Theo; she wanted to keep it light. "Theo, when I bought this ruin, people referred to me as Don Quixote. You know who that makes you?"

"Who?" shouted Christina.

Grinning, Theo bowed. "Sancho Panza, at your service."

"You have a lot in common with him—you're courageous, loyal,

a great companion. You're also a terrific craftsman and problem
solver. We wouldn't be here without you. Thank you."

Georgia jumped to her feet. "I also have a toast—to our host-
ess. May you have many, many years of happiness in your new
home and may you invite us often to share in your tranquility."

Tranquility. Alexis leaned against the cell wall and cried. If
only Easter Sunday hadn't been followed by Easter Monday.

Once her Athenian guests had departed Monday morning,
Alexis, Yiannis and Christina drove back to the press. Theo, pre-
paring the ground for the last flagstones, handed Yiannis a shovel.
Koukla, the mother cat, ran up to greet Alexis and Christina, meowing insistently.

"Koukla certainly loves you," Alexis said.

"I love her *and* the boy kitten." Christina was angling for a gift
of a kitten, but Helen had said no, too much confusion at the
house with another baby imminent.

Alexis took her godchild by the hand. "Let's take a walk." They
set off up the path, Koukla in the lead, still plaintively meowing.
They talked about the summer, Alexis subtly trying to find out
how Christina felt about Olga coming.

Christina was noncommittal. She took a little skip and bounded
ahead. Suddenly she vaulted the low stone wall just above the
road, chasing after Koukla, who was now yowling. Christina
screamed. Alexis tore after her.

Under an olive tree lay the orange kitten, stiff, paws tight in a
ball, eyes open, staring at the sky.

"Alexi, he's hurt," Christina shouted.

Alexis saw the kitten was dead. Trembling, she took her windbreaker from around her waist, placed the kitten in it. "Christina,
run back to the *liotrivi* and get help. Go."

Christina took off, yelling for her father. Holding the lifeless
bundle in her arms, Alexis stumbled toward the house.

Yiannis and Christina came running. Yiannis searched Alexis'
face, understood.

"Christina *mou*, you and your papa have to go to the harbor right away and get your Mama to find my book on cats. She can read me the instructions on how to make the kitten better. Okay?"

"Yes." She pulled her father toward the car.

When Theo caught sight of Alexis kneeling on the ground, he sprinted over from his cement pile. She opened the windbreaker. "He's dead."

She choked up, ran into the house. Theo followed.

"Where are the other kittens?" she asked, anxiously looking around.

"I haven't seen them since the party."

She grabbed his arm. "Please help me look."

They ran back to the field where Koukla, still yowling, led them straight to the others. Theo picked up the kittens gently, one in each hand, held them against his chest.

"They're barely alive." His eyes combed the area. "Under the tree, Alexi. Get that piece of meat. I'm sure it's poisoned. These cats must throw up what they ate."

He took off. When she got back to the terrace, he was balling up salt in his hand. "This can be dangerous, but if we don't do it, they'll die for certain. Don't look."

She had to watch. He stuffed the balls of salt down the kittens' throats. With shudders, one, then the other, raised itself slightly and vomited up tiny pieces of meat.

"Alexi, put milk in the dropper. We need to calm their stomachs. I'll bring them inside."

The kittens were terribly weak, but Alexis got several drops of milk down them.

"I don't know if we cleaned out all the poison. If we did, they should be all right."

She wiped her streaming eyes with the sleeve of her sweatshirt.

He reached out for her, held her against his chest. "The Koutsos cousins did this. Panayiotis was in Pygi this weekend."

"They're animals," she sobbed. "Some day I'm going to kill them, murder them in cold blood."

She pulled away, stroked the two gray kittens, who were barely breathing. Koukla took over, licking them vigorously, as she nestled down beside them.

"Alexi, shall we bury the kitten?"

She nodded, unable to speak.

Outside, Alexis watched Theo dig a deep hole under an olive tree at the edge of the terrace. He lay the kitten down, covered him with branches.

She stood staring at the hole. "Theo. Help me."

He lay down his shovel, gripped her shoulder. "This creature is returning to mother earth who will embrace him as you did, Alexi."

Crying again, Alexis rested her head on his shoulder. "Those are beautiful words, Theo, but beauty means nothing in this place." She bowed her head. "I can't take any more."

"Alexi, you need rest. We'll talk later." He led her inside, handed her his pillow, went back out.

Exhausted, Alexis curled up on the floor next to the kittens. She felt cold rage forming, like a block of ice, in her chest. She would not be a victim; she'd fight back. Sooner or later, she'd avenge herself against the real animals.

Alexis curled up on the floor of her cell. She'd said it then and meant it—she'd kill the Koutsos cousins in cold blood. Had she? What had happened? Her brain was bursting. Mounds of blood-ied fur flashed before her eyes. She was losing touch with reality.

The matron knocked, ran over. "My dear, what are you doing on the floor? You can't stay there."

Alexis blinked several times as she pushed her way back to the present. "The light was hurting my eyes."

The matron helped her up, caressed her hair. "It's past mid-night. You'd better rest up for tomorrow."

Alexis trembled, anticipating the return of the dream. "I'm so upset. I doubt I'll sleep unless I take a pill."

"Then take one." The matron reached for the bottle on the table. "Let me get you some water."

"I can't be groggy in the morning."

"I'll wake you early. I'll bring you as much coffee as you need. It's better to sleep now."

"Thank you. You've been so good to me. When I get out of here, I'm going to do something wonderful for you."

"What I want is to see you free."

She gave the matron a grateful look. "I'll work on it."

CHAPTER 8

Even with the pill, Alexis tossed restlessly, her dreams, vague and shadowy. At two a.m., she awoke to the clanging of an imaginary church bell.

By morning, she was experiencing terrifying mood swings from breathless elation that her wait would soon be over to grinding despair that Maria and Nikos had not yet arrived.

She dressed for the hearing. The navy skirt barely hung on her hips, made her look like a waif, but she didn't care. She packed her towel, bath things, and dirty clothes in Georgia's duffel bag, carried the bag to the door of the cell. Unable to find anything else to do, she slumped at the table, an unopened novel before her.

At ten-fifteen, the matron finally unlocked the door and cheerfully beckoned.

Despite the heat, Alexis shivered when she glimpsed Maria and Nikos in the consultation room, seemingly agitated, hunched over a document. Maria looked up at last. She flashed a smile, gave Alexis a thumb's-up.

"*Kalimera sas.*" Alexis sat down opposite her lawyers, clasped her hands on the table, praying the smile signified more than encouragement. "Is there news?"

"Excellent news, Alexi." Nikos removed his glasses, leaned back in his chair.

"They arrested Ioannidis?" she said, her heart pumping with joy.

"No. His alibi held like glue."

"Then what?"

"This is no longer a murder case."

She stared at him, dazed. "I don't understand."

"A half hour ago, we finally got the autopsy report. Now we know why they didn't want to release it. Loukas died of a massive heart attack, not a blow to the head."

Alexis sat motionless, unsure of his meaning. "Couldn't the blow have caused the heart attack?"

"Impossible. The extensive damage to the heart shows the coronary preceded the blow. If the blow had knocked him out or killed him, the heart would have been more intact."

"No bullet holes?"

"Not one."

Alexis gripped the edge of the table. "I think I get what you're saying, but please spell it out."

Maria jumped in. "Loukas died of natural causes. After his heart attack, someone struck him on the head and dumped his body in the orchard. To frame you, make it *look* like murder. There's no way you would have struck that blow. Why would you try to murder a dead man?"

"So I'm free?"

"Almost," Nikos said. "We have the hearing at twelve."

Alexis still hesitated. "What about Theo?"

"Much as they wanted to, the police never arrested him. Helen swore he was in Nemea the whole time. He didn't break in several sessions of questioning."

Alexis smiled to herself. "He knows something about interrogations. When can I see him?"

"Not for some time, Alexi." Nikos lowered his voice. "The police are still convinced he was there during the fire. They don't believe you and Yiannis could have cut down all those trees. They'd love to pin something on Theo. They won't stop trying."

Bile rose in her throat. "Immigrants make perfect scapegoats."

"You can talk to Theo by phone, but no visiting. We don't want to give the police any reason to suspect you're covering for him."

"Now, the hearing," Maria said. "You feel prepared?"

Alexis nodded.

"Good. The guards will bring you to the court. Afterwards, we'll go to lunch and celebrate."

Celebrating seemed inconceivable. The time in jail had gotten to her.

Back in her cell, she took a minute to collect herself. Despite all the Koutsos cousins had put her through, she felt relieved Loukas had not been murdered. Who could have been so macabre as to mutilate his corpse?

She took a last look around, a bit anxious about leaving. She hated the place, but it felt strangely safe. Now she had to testify—and protect Theo.

No, that was the wrong way to think about it. She had to eliminate Theo from her thoughts. He wasn't there. He stayed in Nemea with Helen.

*   *   *

An armed guard led Alexis into the cheerless courtroom, ushered her to a seat at a bare wooden table. He firmly stationed himself an arm's-length away.

Nikos and Maria hurried in, took seats on either side of her, spread out their papers. Georgia swept in next, her red bouffant hair sedately pinned in a chignon. She settled in her place behind them, reached over to rub Alexis' shoulder, and whispered, "Don't worry, Alexi *mou*."

Across the way, Nitsa, the grieving widow in a tight black dress and lace veil covering her brassy hair, huddled with female comforters. Toward the back, Panayiotis, in a black polo shirt, collar turned up, lounged against the wall, occasionally murmuring to a gaunt young man beside him, who sported a pointed goatee and metallic jacket.

Maria leaned over to Alexis. "Nikos will start. You keep an eye on Nitsa. I'm going to watch Panayiotis. I'll explain later."

The three black-robed judges filed in, took their seats in straight-backed wooden chairs on the high platform. The beak-nosed prosecutor, in a rust-colored sport jacket, a confident look on his face, strode forward. Nikos joined him in front of the judges, held up the autopsy report, spoke quietly for several minutes. He then passed the report to the chief judge. Alexis strained to pick up his words but, with his back to the courtroom, his speech was inaudible.

The frowning judge pulled out his half-glasses, studied the autopsy report. He raised his eyebrows, quickly conferred with his colleague on each side, then passed the report to the prosecutor who angrily flipped through it. The judge motioned the lawyers back to their places.

Nikos began his presentation—a request for the defendant's immediate release based on the definitive autopsy results. Nitsa's head snapped up. She craned her neck forward. As Nikos explained that a heart attack, not a blow, had killed Loukas, Nitsa leaned dramatically back into the arms of the old woman next to her. Ever so subtly, she peered around to catch a glimpse of Panayiotis. Alexis looked, too. His nostrils flaring and his eyes darting around the room, Panayiotis appeared furious. Nitsa returned to her role of grieving widow.

The prosecutor argued for keeping Alexis in jail. While he conceded it was no longer a murder case, he insisted there were still serious unanswered questions: who struck the blow and why; how Loukas' body ended up in Serros.

Maria sprang to her feet. "Dear members of the court, these questions have nothing to do with our client. They are matters for the police. To my knowledge, we are not gathered here to reduce the police workload."

Alexis caught Panayiotis turning away in disgust.

"There is no basis for detaining my client," Maria continued sternly. "For five days, she has been imprisoned on suspicion of murder without a shred of evidence. Now, we learn there was no murder. Rather, there was a death by natural causes and the mysterious appearance of a mutilated corpse."

Maria turned to face Nitsa, subtly casting suspicion on her. "Mr. Koutsos' widow attested her husband was alive and well in Athens on Saturday morning when my client was three hours away in Serros, as numerous witnesses have sworn. My client remained in Serros fighting a fire that reached the area Saturday evening. She could not possibly have transported Mr. Koutsos' body from Athens to the olive orchard."

Maria turned back to the judges. "Who did and why is an important question, but it has no bearing on the petition before you. In that regard, I ask you to release my client immediately."

She clasped her hands in front of her, leaned back on her spike heels, and waited.

The judges conferred again. The chief judge looked irritably at the prosecutor who shrugged. The judge slapped down the file and ordered Alexis to stand. He apologized for any inconvenience she'd been caused, then instructed the prosecutor to release the prisoner forthwith. Georgia reached over, gathered Alexis in her arms.

By the time Alexis, a free woman at last, looked his way, Panayiotis had disappeared. Nitsa, holding her head in her lap and feigning shock, continued her near stellar performance.

* * *

The Mikrolimano harbor restaurant, shielded from the sun by a green and white striped awning, its white tablecloths fluttering in the breeze, would have made an appealing postcard. Glittering light danced on the water; elegant schooners swayed at anchor.

Alexis drank in the scene, inhaled deeply. "You have no idea how delicious the sea air smells." She held up her wine glass. "To the three people who got me through one of the worst experiences of my life."

"*Bravo* to you," Georgia said. "You showed great courage, never panicked or wavered."

She'd come close. "At least, on the outside."

They clinked glasses.

"You were remarkable, Alexi, the ideal client," Maria said. "I don't want to spoil the celebration, but I wonder if we can make this a working lunch."

Georgia waved to the waiter to place their orders. "What are we working on?"

"Who framed Alexis."

"Does it really matter? Let's leave Alexis in peace."

Nikos shook his head vigorously. "Someone went to a great deal of trouble—carried a three hundred pound corpse to an island and up a hillside—for a reason."

"It matters, Aunt Georgia," Alexis said. "If someone tried to frame me for murder, he could do a lot worse."

"She's right," Nikos said. "It's still a dangerous situation. Moreover, until the perpetrator is found, she'll remain a police suspect." He paused. "Theo even more so."

Georgia sighed. "This is so depressing."

Maria jumped in. "Actually, no. What you two don't know is Nikos and I have been doing some investigating. We've learned some curious things about the charming widow and her devoted cousin by marriage."

"Tell us," Alexis urged.

"We started with the salesgirl in Nitsa's dress shop. The girl dislikes her boss intensely. Nitsa's domineering, demeaning, and tight with money."

"She has crabs in her pockets." Alexis had wanted to use that Greek expression for years.

Maria chortled. "Big crabs. Anyway, once when the salesgirl worked late and once when she returned to the shop for a package she'd forgotten, she saw a truck unloading cartons. They were not definitely not dress cartons, more the size of television sets or cases of liquor. They were stashed in a padlocked storage shed behind the shop. Within a few days, the shed was again unlocked and empty." Maria paused for effect. "Nitsa received the deliveries with someone who fits the description of Panayiotis."

"So they're smugglers." Georgia removed the pins and fluffed out her copper hair. "That has nothing to do with Alexis. Loukas' heart attack got him out of the way. Why turn into a murder?"

Maria pounced. "That's the point. Loukas dies. Nitsa inherits his land, Panayiotis has his. But there's one missing piece—the *liotrivi*. They want it back to have one large property, to live happily ever after."

Georgia frowned. "Panayiotis and Nitsa don't give a damn about Serros. They're too flashy—more Rafina types."

"Maybe it's something else," Nikos said. "Remember our other court case. Panayiotis was enraged a foreigner was living on Koutsos land."

Alexis drummed her fingers on the table. "The great patriot? I'm sorry, but there's got to be more to it."

"You're probably right," Nikos said. "I think Nitsa's the key. If we can get to her somehow . . . "

Georgia crossed her arms in front of her. "After today, they're going to be very careful."

Maria speared the last piece of calamari. "We've got to lull them into a false sense of security, then get proof of their business dealings and relationship."

Alexis felt impatient. "In America, we'd use detectives."

"A waste of money during the summer holidays," Maria said. "Everyone's on vacation—even the criminals."

Nikos waved for the check. "For now, Alexi, go back to Serros. Enjoy your wonderful house, work on your garden, relax. We'll get back on the case after August fifteenth."

"If they come out to Serros?" Alexis scowled at the thought of having them around.

"I doubt they will, but if they do, call us immediately."

"Aha. Easier said than done," Georgia said triumphantly, "until now." She reached for the plastic shopping bag next to her chair, thrust it at Alexis. "I almost gave up, but I finally found an outfit that serves Serros."

"A cellular phone," Alexis exclaimed with delight. "I was thinking of getting one but—"

"The bills come to me. I know you. You'll worry about running up charges, but you'll have to spend the monthly minimum at least. And I'll be able to check on you."

Alexis hugged her. "I'll call you the minute I get home."

Maria cleared her throat. "There's one last thing, Alexi. Theo. He can't come to Serros, and you shouldn't be seen with him in Nemea. It's as much for his protection as yours."

"I understand. I don't want the police tracking him."

"You can call him on your new phone," Georgia said, winking.

"We'll get to the bottom of this," Nikos promised. "It just needs time."

Not too long, Alexis thought. She wanted her name completely cleared, and she wanted to see Theo.

SERROS

CHAPTER 9

Alexis gazed out the window of the hydrofoil, thrilled to see the north end of Serros unscathed by the fire. She'd been chomping at the bit to get back. For two days, Vaso had tried to fatten her up, made sure she got a lot of rest. Alexis had shopped for things for the olive press, received congratulations on her release from friends, but all the time she'd been yearning for her island home.

Now, laden with shopping bags, she joyfully disembarked, threw her arms round Sophia in her summer black, waiting on the pier. It had been only a week since the fire, but she felt like she was returning from a year-long journey. The harbor was busier than she'd ever seen it with every table at the *taverna* filled with visitors.

"It doesn't look like the fire has hurt business," Alexis said.

"It has, Alexi." Sophia took some of her packages. "Many of these people planned to camp on the south shore which is all burned. They're leaving early."

"Too bad."

"We'll survive. *Pedi mou*, you're coming to my house for lunch before going up to the *liotrivi*." She pulled Alexis by the arm.

"I'd love to, but I have no food at the press. I have to get to the shops before they close."

"Don't worry. Popi filled your refrigerator. She and Thanos are coming by at three to drive you home."

"As usual, you've taken care of everything. Thank you."

At Sophia's, they sat with *yiayia* in the garden under the vine-covered pergola, sipping *retsina* and munching almonds. Alexis floated on clouds of contentment until Sophia brought her down with a thud.

"Alexi *mou*, things have changed a bit around here." Sophia studied her oleanders. "It may be a while until they get back to normal."

"What things?"

"Oh, Alexi, there's terrible gossip about you. Some of the Serrians blame you for Loukas' death."

"That's ridiculous. Loukas died of a heart attack. I had no connection whatsoever. The judge even apologized for detaining me."

"But his head was bashed in. People don't believe it was his heart. The Koutsos family has turned some people against you—you and Theo."

Alexis was outraged. "Then we have to tell them the truth. I'm the one who suffered in jail. It may well be a Koutsos who is responsible."

"Who?"

Alexis couldn't reveal what she knew about Panayiotis and Nitsa, even to Sophia. Everything depended on taking them by surprise. "Sophia, we've got to stop this immediately."

"There's nothing we can do. It will all die down eventually. If you just keep to yourself for a few weeks, the town will forget the whole thing."

Yiayia nodded her head in agreement. "Alexi, you must remember you're a foreigner. The Koutsos are from here. There will always be people who take their side, no matter what."

Speechless, Alexis retreated to the kitchen. She poured a glass of water, gulped it down, then another. She should have listened to her Athenian friends—she'd never fit in with the village mentality. How naive she'd been. How she'd romanticized island life. Well, she wasn't going to be the perennial scapegoat. She'd finish out the summer, put the olive press up for sale, sell it to some obnoxious city folks the locals would *really* dislike.

Sophia peeked into the kitchen. "Alexi, I'm ashamed of the Serrians, but I had to warn you." Her hands clasped in front of her breast, she looked distraught.

"I'm not upset with you," Alexis said with a sigh. "I'm just discouraged. I thought my troubles were over."

Sophia put her arms around Alexis. "It will pass. Shall we have lunch? I made your favorite—*pastitsio*."

Alexis forced a smile. "Yes, let's eat, drink and curse my fate."

* * *

Popi and Thanos came by, the kids and egg crates piled in the back of the truck. Against Popi's steady stream of chatter, no one noticed Alexis' silence. At Popi's, Alexis gathered Koukla and the two kittens up in her arms. "You have no idea how much I missed these creatures."

"They missed you, too, Alexi. We all did."

"Not from what Sophia tells me. She said many people blame me for Loukas' death. What about Pygi?"

Popi turned crimson. "We know the Koutsos better out here, how bad they are. But Panayiotis came while you were in jail and said some ugly things about you. I had words with him."

Alexis groaned. "Thanks for defending me. What was Panayiotis doing besides slandering me?"

"He came with another man, younger, short beard. They spent a lot of time up on the mountain."

"Not working in the olive orchard?"

"No, not that. I don't know what."

"He could have had more poison. I'm going to have to keep the cats inside."

Popi nodded sadly. "It's a good idea, Alexi."

"Popi, my friend Georgia gave me a cellular phone. Here's the number. If you ever see Panayiotis or Nitsa around, will you let me know right away?"

"Of course. I'm so glad I can call you, Alexi. Will you be here all summer?"

"I plan to. Why?"

"I've never let anyone take care of my chickens, but I trust you. Thanos wants to go to his mother's in the Mani for a week."

"I'd be happy to feed the chickens. Just tell me when."

"You can keep all the eggs."

"I couldn't possibly. I'll take them around to the villagers." If they're talking to me, she thought to herself.

*   *   *

The *liotrivi* was the most welcoming thing about Serros, Alexis mused. The stone building, the colorful garden, the winding path—all achingly lovely, all filled with vivid memories of working beside Theo. Only the view from the back—Loukas' blackened orchard—served as a reminder of what she'd been through.

The villagers of Serros be damned. She'd had enough of people; her cats would be her company. After her time in jail, living within her own four walls, with the freedom to do whatever she wanted, felt like an incredible gift. She'd throw herself into gardening and cooking. And she could call Nemea whenever she liked.

She unloaded the van, aired out the house, examined the refrigerator stuffed with local cheeses, eggs, fruit, and vegetables. She took a book and glass of *retsina* out to the garden, tried to keep her mind on her pleasure at being home.

It didn't work. She kept imagining Panayiotis wandering on the mountain, doing his evil deeds, whatever they were. Much as she hated the thought of going up there, she had to find out what he was up to. She'd check out the temple site and the cave in the morning.

The cave. It had been such a powerful experience the first time. On the day she and Theo had finished installing the windows, Alexis, in a light-hearted mood, insisted they take a few hours off. She'd learned about the cave from Nassos, had been wanting to explore it, but not alone.

They set out with sandwiches, a thermos of coffee, and a flashlight. At the temple site, they circled behind the church, picked their way among the sharp rocks and prickly shrubs to the base of the cliff, a stunning collage of ocher and chartreuse lichens.

Alexis searched for the mouth of a cave. "It's solid rock."

"If the Serrians used this as a hide-out from pirates," Theo said, "the entrance would be well camouflaged. Over there. That crevice." He crossed to a gash in the cliff face behind several large boulders, aimed the flashlight inside. "There's a passage through here. Let's take a look. Stay close behind me so you can see."

Alexis was happy to have Theo take the lead. The narrow passage wound through the cliff wall for about twenty yards. After the second turn, there was no daylight. She grabbed his belt, her heart pumping faster, seemingly louder, with each step.

Theo reached back for her arm, gently guided her forward. "Look." He arced light across the high ceiling of a rounded cavern. The sandstone walls were rough like pumice. "Not a bad shelter. Let's see how deep it is."

They moved farther into the cave, which opened wider and wider. Gray-brown bands of light thick with motes of dust filtered through an opening in the roof. Theo shut off the flashlight. The soft light illuminated a large rock formation at the back of the cave. Alexis stopped in awe.

Closer, they discovered a smooth outcropping of rock in the shape of an elongated cupped hand, the size of a human being.

"It looks like a throne for a deity," Alexis murmured. "Or a womb. This is a shrine to the mother goddess. Petros was only half-right. Artemis came later. Wait 'til the archeologists see this."

"Perhaps you should ask the Serrians first," Theo said. "They may not want archeologists up here."

Knowing what she now knew about the small-minded Serrians, Alexis thought, Theo was undoubtedly right. Too bad.

"Theo, this mountain belongs to humankind. The Serrians can't stand in the way of archeology."

"Isn't that what the British say about keeping the Elgin marbles?"

Alexis had stared at him, confounded by his perspective. "I'll have to think about it. For the time being, I'll keep it secret."

"Our secret."

His sudden intimacy had pierced her defensive shell. The cave had remained their secret.

Now, they had another—the fire. She looked around her flowering garden, felt terribly alone.

*   *   *

The next morning Alexis procrastinated about making the climb to the temple. By the time she lay down for her afternoon nap, she admitted to herself she was afraid. She could make it to the top, but she could never make it into the cave. The only way to do it was to get someone to come with her, perhaps Popi after her vacation.

The strange chirp of the cellular woke her. "How are you?" Helen asked. "And how is home?"

"Hi. Home is wonderful." Alexis considered telling Helen about the poisoned atmosphere in Serros, but didn't want to upset her. "How's my godchild and all the rest of the family?"

"We're all fine."

Hesitant to ask about Theo, Alexis said, "How's Olga doing?"

"At first, she retreated into herself. I couldn't get her away from the television for quite a while."

"Now?"

Helen laughed. "She and Christina are working it out. They love and hate each other. They argue, but that means Olga's standing on her own feet."

"Christina's never had any female competition. It may take a while."

"She's coming along. Theo is building the girls a tree house out back. Christina's very happy with that."

Alexis filled with happiness at Theo's name.

Helen cleared her voice. "*Agapi mou*, I called to ask you a favor."

"Anything."

"Can you go to Hydra on Saturday? Overnight?"

"Sure. What are we doing?"

"*We're* not doing anything. I'm due next month. But I can't bear Theo mooning around here any longer. He really wants to see you. I've reserved rooms at Yiannis' aunt's *pension*."

Alexis was speechless. Could she do this? "Have you asked Theo?"

"I don't need to. I just had to check with you. Look, I know the police aren't supposed to find you two together, but they'll never spot you in the summer crowds at Hydra."

"Helen, you are really playing *koumbara*. I wonder—"

"Don't wonder. Even Yiannis approves of my plan. Just be on the ferry to Hydra on Saturday. Go to Evangelia's Guesthouse. Theo will be coming on the three o'clock hydrofoil from Nauplion."

CHAPTER 10

Shading her eyes against the blinding afternoon sun, Alexis searched the still, blue-violet gulf for the hydrofoil. She'd arrived several hours earlier, climbed the narrow streets from Hydra's port to the hillside *pension*, and settled into her simple room. Her bottle of white wine was cooling in Evangelia's refrigerator. The tiny balcony, holding two wooden chairs and a small, round iron table, would be a lovely place to watch the sunset.

Despite the humidity and hordes of tourists, Alexis had walked back down to the port, wandered restlessly through the shops, drunk a coffee frappe in one of the buzzing waterfront cafes. Now, perched high above the harbor on the base of the statue of Miaoulis, the Greek naval hero, she wondered what the next two days would bring.

In Serros, she and Theo had established an easy and close companionship: sharing their views of the world, joking about each other's foibles, reading each other's minds. He'd become her partner in every way except sexually. Could that happen? Early on, they'd dropped their roles as employer and employee. After all, Theo had been more in charge of the restoration than she had. But could they also bridge the cultural divide—nationality, class, life experience? Vaso's warnings echoed in her head.

Hearing a boat's hum, Alexis looked toward the Peloponnesus, caught the yellow hydrofoil skimming over the sea. She sped down the steps to be on the pier when Theo arrived, anxiously scanned the disembarking vacationers, but didn't see him.

"I've missed you, Alexi." He stood before her in a white tennis shirt, khakis, moccasins, and aviator sunglasses. He'd shaved off his beard, his thick blond was cut short.

"Theo, you're transformed. You look like every other tourist."

"That's the idea. I'm incognito." Grinning, he put his hands on her shoulders, kissed her on both cheeks. "Helen took me shopping in Nauplion."

"What happened to the country boy?"

"Too late, Alexi. The country boy has joined the twentieth century."

"So I see. That's a large bag for overnight. You're sure you haven't got my old buddy, Theodoros, tucked in there?"

He slung the bag over his shoulder. "One hundred percent sure."

Alexis quickly understood much had happened in the few weeks since they'd last been together. Theo had always been confident about his abilities, less sure of his direction in life. Now, he seemed to have made a choice—he was going to be a modern Greek.

"What would you like to do?" Alexis asked tentatively. "Have a coffee here in the harbor?"

"Let's go to the *pension*. I want to hear everything that's happened to you."

"Me, too, about you. Shall we drink wine and talk on the balcony?"

"Lead the way."

At the *pension*, Evangelia brought the wine, glasses, and a plate of olives and cheese to Alexis' small balcony. After catching up on Yiannis from Theo, she left, smiling broadly, wishing them a good rest.

Alexis picked up her wine glass. "Here's to my clever friend, Helen. It never occurred to me to meet somewhere else, far from nosy neighbors and suspicious policemen. I suppose it's a small risk but—"

"Helen understood how much I wanted to see you. Alexi, Helen and Yiannis are the best people I've ever known."

"You go first. Tell me about your time there."

Theo described his days in the vineyard, his satisfaction in working for Yiannis, who paid him regular Greek wages. He recounted life in the loving Vassilopoulos household, feeling like a member of the family, learning the niceties of middle class life.

"Like talking on the telephone," he said. "I didn't know about asking the person on the other end how they are, their news, before getting down to business. My family didn't have a phone. On the village phone, we had to talk fast and get off."

She flashed a smile. "I understand."

"And eating," he said. "There's a whole different way with a knife and fork."

Theo held her hand. She felt a rush of pleasure, warmth rising to her cheeks.

"Now tell me about prison," he said.

"Could that wait? I'm feeling so good now."

He gazed at the copper disc spreading its rays on the opaque sea. "Okay, but we have to talk. I have some ideas about what to do next."

Alexis was curious but didn't want to lose the mood of the afternoon. "Do you have winter plans, Theo? Are you taking Olga back to Albania?"

"I don't think so. Her Greek is good enough to start school here. If I can get my parents and brother out as well, I'll rent a house for all of us. I can make enough money to support us. I'll be working with a contractor once Yiannis' harvest is in."

"Everything's falling into place."

"Almost. Thanks to Helen and Yiannis—and you."

"I had nothing to do with it."

He squeezed her hand. "You have more to do with it than you know."

Alexis sensed he was leading up to something.

"You're going back to your school?"

"I'm giving it one more chance. Vaso, Cliff, and I have been elected to run the Faculty Council." She laughed. "The principal is apparently quite upset I've become the faculty spokesperson."

"Sounds like you'll be busy."

"Yes, but I'm not abandoning the *liotrivi*. I intend to come out to Serros every weekend. My biggest dilemma is the cats. I don't think they'll be happy cooped up in an apartment."

"No problem, Alexi. I'll take them for the winter. It'd be good for Olga."

She looked at him, amazed. This man, with so few resources, was once again taking care of her. "You're still doing it."

"Doing what?"

"Being a gift from God."

"The gifts have come to me, Alexi. Your coming to Hydra."

Across the gulf, a rosy backdrop illuminated the mountain ridges. The beauty of the moment, their new openness with each other, Theo's deep concern for her—it all overwhelmed Alexis. She felt her shell opening, surges of emotion like ocean waves sweeping in and out.

Theo faced her. "Alexi, you mentioned risks. I've learned a lot in my life. You've got to take risks for the things you really want."

"You've taken many risks."

"Not the most important—until now." He locked his fingers in hers. "After I left Serros, I realized you'll never know what I feel if I don't tell you. Alexi, you're the first—and only—woman I've ever loved."

"Theo—"

"Wait. I don't expect anything. I only wanted to tell you."

Alexis exhaled deeply before going on. "Over the past couple of months, I've discovered how much my pleasure in life comes from being with you. I've missed you." Alexis felt a strong need to hold him. "I want to see where this takes us."

He broke into a radiant smile, led her by the hand inside. "I want you to be pleased. Tell me if I do something wrong."

"Theo, we've always been good at learning from each other."

From the moment she felt Theo's skin next to hers, Alexis strained to know every part of him. Like a child on Christmas morning tearing into her gifts, she touched, smelled, tasted his hard body. He soon lost his reserve, calling her name over and over as he embraced her. They'd reined in their mutual attraction for so long; now, they gave themselves to it.

The bedsprings creaked loudly, the headboard bumped against the wall. Alexis flashed on how embarrassed Petros, the cool, sophisticated lover, would be by such a scene. She broke out in laughter.

"What is it, Alexi *mou*?"

She ruffled his hair. "I'm wondering what Evangelia will say to Yiannis about all this."

"She's going to tell him I'm your gift from God."

With a surrender she'd never felt before, their bodies merged. She lost all consciousness of physical boundaries, as if all the senses were shared.

They finally slept side by side on the narrow bed.

When Alexis woke, Theo was staring at her face. "Your eyes are cat's eyes, like Koukla's."

"I'm honored." She held his face in her hands, kissed him. "I think I'd like to keep the new Theo, as long as you don't change any more."

"I'll change, Alexi. So will you. I hope we'll change together."

"I've changed a lot in the last few hours. I feel like I'm shedding an old skin. Do you know what I mean?"

"I know there's a wonderful creature underneath." He kissed her neck. "Where am I taking you for dinner?"

Alexis understood he wanted to do something special for her. "I accept your invitation as long as it's my treat next time."

"Helen warned me you'd say that. She also told me where to take you if you don't have any preference."

Helen—the unquestioned *koumbara* of this relationship. Alexis felt blessed. Most everyone else would oppose it. What a joy to have Helen and Yiannis on her side. On their side.

She winked at Theo. "I'm in your most capable hands."

* * *

They walked arm in arm down the cobblestone streets to town. Around a bend, they came upon a pocket garden where they stopped at a stone bench nestled between two fragrant orange trees. Hydra's lights twinkled, sleek white luxury yachts crowded the protected anchorage, and across the gulf, an apricot half moon balanced on the rim of the mountains.

Theo pulled Alexis close. "This is the most wonderful place I've ever been, although it could be the way I feel."

"More wonderful than the Acropolis?"

He looked at her gravely. "For me, it started that day. What about you, Alexi?"

"I can't decide. Was it staining or varnishing?"

"Seriously. Tell me."

Thinking back to their days at the *liotrivi*, suddenly she knew. "When we buried the kitten. I was full of hate that day. You reached me deep inside, helped me feel love, even with all the evil in the world. I knew I cared for you then." She let go of tears held back too long.

He wiped her cheeks, gently pulled her up, and led her toward town.

At the posh *taverna* beyond the harbor, Theo chose a table overlooking the sea, far from the other diners. He ordered white wine, Greek salad and octopus first, then grilled fish. Extravagant, as he wanted it.

Theo filled their wine glasses. "Now, tell me about jail. I know some things from Helen and Yiannis, but I want to hear it from you."

Reluctantly, Alexis described her arrest, the painful days in the detention center, the results of the autopsy and hearing, the admonitions to stay away from him.

He looked puzzled. "I still don't understand how they could hold you. They had no evidence."

She'd decided not to mention the police finding the gun or the old woman seeing him at the harbor. She didn't want him feeling in any way responsible. "You know Serros. Loukas and Panayiotis made sure everyone knew about the lawsuit and the

tension between them and me. The Serrians had no problem believing I'd done Loukas in—still don't. In the village mindset, you
take revenge on your enemy, *especially* if he's a neighbor."

"Not so different from Albania."

Alexis leaned over and hugged him. "Anyway, the prosecutor
apparently believed I'd confess if he held me long enough. Fortu-
nately, I had Maria and Nikos."

"They were wonderful to me, too, Alexi."

"They're not quitting." Alexis shared what the lawyers had
discovered about Nitsa and Panayiotis, then reported on Panayiotis'
recent visit to Serros. At the end of her tale, she felt strangely
deflated. "I'm now convinced Panayiotis is behind this whole business, but there's little to go on. Some months ago he and Nitsa
handled contraband. How can that help now?"

"It does. We know they're criminals, working together. We
know Panayiotis is out to get you. There's a connection somewhere
to the olive press. We need to watch those two."

"Detectives will be useless if the smuggling has stopped."

"Detectives aren't necessary. I'm going to Athens."

Alexis gasped. "To do what?"

"To catch Panayiotis at his game."

"You can't. You're a suspect."

"To the police. As far as we know, Panayiotis doesn't even know
what I look like. Remember, I was out of sight the day of the court
case against Loukas."

"What about Easter? He could have been in Serros other times,
too, lurking around without your seeing him."

"That's possible." Theo seemed determined to be reasonable.
"But he won't recognize me this time. I don't look the same."

He not only looks different, he also behaves differently, Alexis
thought.

"Anyway, I'm not going to confront him," Theo continued.
"I'm going to spy on him. I'll leave for Athens from here."

"That explains the duffel bag."

"Yes. I knew before I came here I'd have to do this."

Alexis sat quietly, her emotions pulling her in opposite directions. Part of her said to stop him. What if Panayiotis caught on? Another part was yearning for action. She couldn't sit out the summer just waiting for Panayiotis to show up. The sooner they got the bastard, the sooner their names would be cleared. "In that case, I'm going with you."

To her surprise, he agreed. "Good. I'm going to need help."

"My Athens apartment is sublet until the end of August, but Vaso's away. We could stay at her place. I have the key."

Theo chuckled, pushed back a strand of her hair. "You're a brave woman, Alexi, but I don't think Athens is ready for us yet. I'll stay with my friends."

He was right. The two of them staying anywhere would create a stir. Even among strangers, they'd have no chance at anonymity. And when word got back to Lincoln, as, so far, everything had . . .

"Okay," she said. "Can we accomplish anything when everyone's out of town?"

"Nitsa won't be traveling. The forty days of mourning aren't up. I doubt Panayiotis would go anywhere without her."

"True love?"

Theo laughed. "More likely he doesn't trust her."

The waiter was noisily clearing a table nearby, sending a message.

"Are we ready to go, Theo?"

He nodded, started to get up.

"You'd better signal for the check."

He grinned at her, waved to the waiter. "I'll soon have it all figured out." Theo took out his battered wallet.

"I have to return to Serros tomorrow. I'll come to Athens with the van the next day. Theo, promise me you won't do anything without me."

"I can wait a day for you." He studied the check, proudly plunked down money. "But only a day."

She didn't believe for a minute he'd sit on his hands until she got there.

CHAPTER 11

Rattled by honking drivers, Alexis maneuvered her van off the ferry at Piraeus. Seeing Theo waving from the pier immediately improved her mood. She pulled up, pushed open the passenger door. "*Yia sou*. Let's get away from these madmen. I hope you don't have any plans for today."

"No, Alexi *mou*. Why?"

The possessive was new. She liked it. "We're going to Sounion. Georgia has something she wants to discuss."

On the phone, Alexis had hinted broadly about the turn in her relationship with Theo. Georgia had hooted with glee.

"Why are you smiling?" Theo said.

"I was thinking about Georgia. We were once at an awful party at Diana's, Petros' mother, where a group of people was discussing immigration. Diana's next-door neighbor carried on about all the new crime in Greece—Bulgarian call girl rings in the north, Russian prostitutes in Glyfada."

"Don't forget the Albanian mafia."

"Indeed. Another woman had just returned from Skiathos where several foreign maids had been raped. She wanted to put the maids under curfew. Georgia said the women weren't to blame, but the people who hired them and raped them, possibly one and the same. The group went into shock as Georgia dragged me away."

"I see why you like her."

"I adore her. I'm glad you'll get to see her home. We'll drive down the Attica coast. It used to be beautiful, but now it's mostly urban sprawl."

"Too bad—not like Serros."

"You really like the country. I'd have thought, after Albania, you'd be seduced by city lights."

"The city is good for visiting, but not for living."

"That's just what we say in America." She turned onto the coast road. "What do you like so much about the country?"

"Dealing with nature. It's a good antidote for people. The communists forced me to become an outdoor man, but I'm not sorry."

"You and Yiannis are both nature boys. You have a lot in common."

"We do." He squeezed her leg. "We both like American girls."

Amazing, Alexis thought, we're becoming a couple. It had been a long time coming, but now they did it easily. "Well, as you know from our last city excursion, this American doubles as tour guide. On the way to Georgia's, we'll visit the Temple to Poseidon."

"I'll be the best educated Albanian in Greece."

"You already are."

* * *

Georgia's two-story Alpine chalet nestled in a pine grove above the coast road. From her second-floor veranda, there was a postcard perfect view of Cape Sounion. The dying sun set the white marble columns of the temple ablaze.

Alexis leaned on the iron railing. "Aunt Georgia, you've created a breathtaking environment."

Georgia, in a billowing yellow caftan, stopped fussing with the tray of drinks and looked at the sunset. "Petros found this land for me when he was a student."

Theo turned around to examine the chalet. "But the house design is yours."

"How did you guess? The people around here with big Mediterranean villas were angry when I put up this place, said it was the wrong style, not on the right scale. But it's invisible in the trees. By now, they've gotten used to me."

"My house in Albania is surrounded by pine trees."

"Come here any time you get homesick, Theo. Bring Olga."

He looked pleased.

"Aunt Georgia," Alexis said, "I can't stand the mystery any longer. What do you want to discuss?"

"Ah, yes." She fixed her gaze on Alexis. "I did something you may not approve of."

"Confess."

"I went to see Nitsa."

"Nitsa? Loukas' wife? Why?"

"To make a deal. I was sure I had her figured out. The woman has a profound love of money. I offered to buy her olive orchard."

"Why?"

"Let me finish. As you can imagine, Nitsa wasn't pleased to see me at her front door. She lives near here in the summer—in Varkiza. I went mid-morning to miss Panayiotis."

Georgia paused, seemed to ponder something.

"And?" Alexis pressed.

"I said I wanted to buy Loukas' property, that I liked Serros, might want to build there some day. Some truth to that. I asked the price."

"I'm sure it was astronomical."

"Definitely not a bargain, especially considering the condition. But that wasn't the point. I told her I agreed, but only if she'd give me an explanation of how Loukas' corpse got to Serros."

"What'd she say to that?"

"She looked upset. I reminded her how much money we were talking about. She said she'd let me know."

"Aunt Georgia, I deeply appreciate what you're trying to do, but—"

"We won't argue because it's not going to happen. Nitsa called back the same evening. She said something quite strange." Georgia looked off into the distance again. "She'd obviously spoken to Panayiotis. I'd been expecting her to say she couldn't give me a statement. I was sure she'd try to sell me the property anyway.

When she said it wasn't for sale at any price, I was astonished."

Georgia turned back to them, her eyes squinting in concentration. "And the *way* she said it, with such regret. *She* wants to sell, but Panayiotis won't let her. I'm sure of this."

Theo jumped up, started pacing. "It fits with an idea I've been working on." He swung his chair around, sat astride it. "When Alexis bought the *liotrivi*, Loukas pressured her to buy his land. He tried everything—closing the road, blocking the window."

"You forget Loukas also scared off all the workmen," Alexis broke in.

His face lit in a smile. "I didn't forget. How could I? Anyway, at Easter, everything changed. Poisoning cats is not pressure, but terror. Loukas and his partner wouldn't have done that. It would never result in a business deal. It had to be Panayiotis. But why?"

"Panayiotis hates foreigners," Alexis said.

"It has to be more than that. Next he tried to frame you for murder. Why? Once Loukas died, he could have the area to himself—except for you. Panayiotis wants you out of the way."

"Why is Alexis in the way?" Georgia said.

"I think he's discovered a use for the *liotrivi*. The best way to get it back was to send Alexis to jail."

Alexis guessed where Theo was heading. "Are you suggesting Panayiotis might need a storage place? Some place remote?"

Georgia slapped the table. "The little side business. Serros would be a marvelous hideaway."

"There's something you both need to know," Theo said. "My fisherman friend, Vassilis, who helped me get away after the fire, told me, from time to time, he sees a high speed luxury yacht in a cove at the south end of the island. A cabin cruiser comes along, loads cargo onto the yacht, then they both disappear."

Georgia couldn't contain herself. "Smuggling on the high seas! What and where?"

"It's probably passing through Greek waters to other ports. If it were meant for Greece, they'd deliver somewhere on the coast. Could be heroin or hashish, from Turkey, say, to France."

Alexis frowned. "We have no way of proving it."

"Yet," Theo intoned.

"We're not going to chase after drug dealers. It's far too dangerous."

"We'll discuss it later."

She tensed. He obviously didn't understand the risks. It was a big leap from tracking Panayiotis' and Nitsa's trade in stolen tv sets to pursuing drug traffickers. She hoped he'd be sensible.

"Why didn't Panayiotis offer to buy back the *liotrivi*?" Georgia asked.

"He'd have to show his hand," Theo said. "The villagers would be very curious why he suddenly wanted it."

"He also knows I wouldn't sell. He must really want it, though, to frame me for murder."

"I'm confused," Georgia said. "Why doesn't he buy some other place in Serros to store things?"

"Same problem—people becoming suspicious," Alexis said. "I know the Serrians."

"Then on some other island."

"There's something special about Serros."

"Whatever he's up to," Theo said, turning to face them, "we'll catch him at it."

Alexis bit her lip. "Not a good idea. We can't possibly take on the Greek connection."

Georgia rose from the table. "Listen, you two. Let's take a break. I want you to relax and enjoy the lobsters my housekeeper prepared."

"Lobsters!" Alexis was eager to change the subject. "I adore them. Theo?"

He looked like his thoughts were elsewhere. "Never tasted them."

Georgia clapped her hands. "What fun. Let me get them. You have to extract them from their shells, you know." She glided off to the kitchen with the tray.

Alexis came over to Theo. "You'll enjoy this. Georgia will have

all the equipment—nutcrackers, little forks that work like picks."
She nuzzled his neck. "It's a bit like stone work."

* * *

Driving back to Athens, Alexis resurrected the issue they'd buried
earlier. "Theo, if we're right about Panayiotis' new activities, we're
up against professionals. It's better to take this to the police."

"With what we have?" he scoffed.

"What do you propose?"

"I'll follow Panayiotis wherever he goes tomorrow, the day after, and the day after. He'll soon lead me to his operation."

"You don't even know where to find him."

"I got his address yesterday from Maria. He's installed himself
in Loukas' old office. I'm going to find some way into it."

Alexis was miffed he'd acted without her. "You called Maria?
She's in on this?"

"You know Maria."

Alexis certainly did. The woman was lucky she had Nikos to
keep her out of trouble.

She swerved over to the curb and parked. "Theo, I've just reconnected with you; I don't want to lose you again."

"I'm planning to wear a disguise, stay in the background."

She gripped the steering wheel. "If you insist on this, I'm coming along. You need an accomplice, the van, someone who can call
the police if—"

"In Albania, I'd say no, and that would be the end of it. I get
the feeling that if I try that, you'll throw me out of the car."

"Going a hundred kilometers an hour."

He drummed his fingers on the dashboard. "What would you
wear for a disguise?"

"You won't recognize me. Meet me at the Omonia underground train station tomorrow at nine. We'll go straight to Loukas'
office. *If* you can find me."

CHAPTER 12

Old newspapers and juice cartons littered the ground at Alexis'
feet. Nauseated from the stale air of the underground station, she
concentrated on the faces of commuters disembarking from steamy
trains, dragging themselves to the nearest exit. Not the usual morning crush. Much of Athens had already abandoned the sweltering
city for the summer holiday.

"Girl, what time is it?" A mechanic in work clothes smeared
with grease stood beside her.

Alexis raised her wrist. "Nine-fifteen."

He moved closer, smelled like motor oil. "Have coffee with me."

"No. Go away."

"Why not? You need me. I can tell."

"Get away from me or I'll yell for that guard over there."

"Don't do that, Alexi."

She spun around.

Theo pulled off his filthy cap, rubbed the stubble on his face.
"The dirt helps." He winked. "You're looking beautiful as ever."

Alexis had pinned up her hair under a white silk scarf, added
huge black sunglasses and gold hoops, painted her mouth a volup-
tuous shocking pink. A black, tight, sleeveless top and short denim
skirt completed the disguise.

"You recognized me."

"You don't look like Alexis, but you're still the best looking
woman around." He nodded toward the Athinas Street exit. "Let's
go. Where's your van?"

"Nearby. In the central market garage."

"Okay. We don't need it now. Later, maybe."

They easily found the side street where Loukas' office was located. Alexis stopped in a *cafeneion* on the corner, while Theo, toolbox in hand, went to poke around the building. When she saw him enter the front door, her stomach clenched.

A minute later, a bearded young man in a black tee shirt came out, climbed in the back of a small blue truck parked at the curb, then emerged again holding a wooden crate. He re-entered the building. Although a block away, Alexis was pretty sure he was the guy with Panayiotis in the courtroom. Panayiotis was probably inside.

She needed to warn Theo, but couldn't parade around this neighborhood without attracting attention. She stood up to get the truck's license plate number, couldn't see anything from that distance except a red and white sticker, the kind displayed by scuba divers.

Alexis needed the plate number. She walked as briskly as possible in her high-heeled sandals down the opposite side of the street, ducked into the electrical supply shop across from the truck. While the shop owner was in the back getting her fuses, she studied the truck through the filthy window. Faint letters on the side read Glyfada Dive Center. She noted down the license plate, purchased the fuses, headed back to the *cafeneion*.

Just as the waiter came for her order, Alexis saw Theo, head down, sprint up the street. She dashed out, caught up with him at the edge of the meat market. "What happened in there?" she said, panting.

"Panayiotis is going with two guys to Glyfada."

"To the dive center."

"How'd you know?"

"It's on the truck. Should we go out there?"

He nodded. "They're meeting someone."

They hurried to the garage.

"Theo, one of those guys was at the court hearing with Panayiotis."

"Then Panayiotis wasn't arranging diving lessons."

The traffic was light. They were soon breezing down Vougliameni Avenue toward the seaside suburb.

"Alexi, I'm betting the dive center has a cabin cruiser that's occasionally used for other purposes, say, deliveries."

Her eyes widened. "Did your fisherman friend ever note the names of the boats he saw?"

"I don't know. I'll call Vassilis later. Hey, there's the sign to Glyfada."

"The next turn-off is better—takes us right to the harbor."

She swung off the four-lane road onto a tree-shaded street lined with luxurious villas behind iron gates. At the coast road, she crossed over to the harbor. The Glyfada Dive Center, a small operation, stood at the north end of the bay.

"I don't see the truck," Alexis said. "Maybe we beat them here."

"Maybe. Park over by that restaurant."

They sat wordlessly for ten minutes, watching the dive center which was strangely quiet for summertime.

Theo grunted in frustration. "They're not coming here. Let's go. They may be out on the pier."

"Would you mind explaining—"

"Not now," he snapped, then pointed. "Park down there, by those trees, facing the water."

She did as he told her, torn between curiosity and irritation. When she stopped the car, he pointed again. "Halfway down the pier on the right, a twenty meter boat with radar on top. The truck's in front."

Alexis removed her sunglasses, squinted. "God, Theo. We've found their transport."

He grimaced. "Now, we catch them at work."

"Oh, no. We give this information to the Coast Guard."

"And say what? There's this guy, Panayiotis, who has friends from a dive shop. They know people with a yacht. If you watch them long enough, you *may* find out they're smugglers."

She didn't have an answer.

"We've got to find out when and where they go, catch them in the act. From all this activity, I'd say they're leaving soon."

"We can't sit here until they sail. Once they take off, how do we catch them?"

He leaned back, frowning, watching through the windshield. "I need to get to know the crew."

She stared at him, anxiety mounting. They'd be on to Theo. Albanians and yachts didn't mix. As they sat in silence, Panayiotis, the young guy with the goatee, and another man in a red baseball cap climbed off the yacht and into the truck. The truck sped down the pier, hurtled off in the direction of Athens.

Alexis exhaled deeply, began a half-monologue. "I've talked my way into situations before. I'm sure I could get on the boat, especially in this outfit."

"I'm sure you can, but can you get off?"

"No one will recognize me. I'll just chat up the crew. Find out when they're sailing, and where. Then I leave."

"Then you leave pronto. I'll be right here. I'll honk loud if I see the truck coming back."

"What then? I dive into the sea? There'd better not be any truck."

*   *   *

The *Frederika*, home port Valletta, was getting a thorough scrubdown. Two crew members in jeans—one brandishing a mop, the other polishing brass—paid no attention to Alexis as she strolled past. She'd have to engage them directly. She turned around, sauntered back, feigning confusion.

"Hello? Excuse me? Can you tell me where the *Paradise* is anchored? It's supposed to be on this pier, but I don't see it anywhere."

The slight, pasty crewman with the mop shrugged.

Alexis persisted. "Do you have a directory? I can't just keep circling the harbor."

"Only the harbormaster has a list."

"Can I borrow your phone to call him?"

The other crew member—six feet plus, at least two hundred fifty pounds, a bushy red beard—came over. "You can call from the bridge. Just take off those shoes." He spoke Greek with a foreign accent.

Alexis pulled off her sandals. "Thank you." She reached for his extended hand. "Where do I go?"

He kept her hand, led her to a ladder. "Up here."

"This is a beautiful boat. Who's Frederika?"

"The owner's daughter."

Keep playing dumb. "And where's Valletta?"

"Malta, the island of knights and pirates."

She laughed flirtatiously. "Which are you?"

"Guess."

"You may be a pirate, but you're not Maltese."

"No, the boat's registered there. We're from Bremen."

They stepped onto the bridge. The cabin was high-tech, all computer screens and digital gadgets, like a Hollywood set for a science fiction film.

"All these instruments," Alexis said. "You must sail around the world."

"Mostly the Mediterranean, but we make the best time, every time."

The crewman called the harbormaster on the radio, passed her the handset.

"Hello? I'm looking for a boat called *Paradise*. Can you tell me where it's located?" Alexis listened, then rolled her eyes. "It must be here. I had an appointment, a sailing party starting at three. Pier 6, Mikrolimano."

She faked surprise, dropping her mouth open. "Piraeus? Not Glyfada? Damn. Okay, thanks."

She gave back the handset. "I'm in the wrong place."

"Not necessarily." The sailor eyed her. "We could have a party here."

Alexis gave him a seductive look. If she played her cards right, she could probably get the whole story, the sailing, itinerary. She pulled off her scarf and shook out her long hair. "You sailing somewhere?"

He came over, rested his hand on her shoulder, rubbed her neck. "Not for a few days, but we don't need to go anywhere. We can party on board."

Alexis stepped back; his body odor was sickening. "I want to go somewhere. Where are you going when you do go?"

"Can't say. But we can party tonight. You bring a friend for Franz."

"Maybe. Franz?"

"My mate. He's German, too, but he speaks good Greek, like you. You English?"

Alexis hid her knowledge of German. An English identity would be just fine. "I'm Lisa. I've been here for eight years; I'm half-Greek by now. What's your name?"

"Kurt."

"No last name?"

"Just Kurt. You wanna drink?"

"Why not?"

He stroked her hair, led her into the salon. Whoever had decorated the top deck favored garish shades of turquoise, yellow and orange. Kurt put Iglesias on the sound system, poured two beers.

Alexis went straight to work. "Could I have a tour of the boat?"

"There's nothing to see," Kurt said impatiently. "The cabin and galley are down one deck, below that the engine room."

"There must be a bathroom. I desperately need one."

"This way. The head's in the cabin."

She followed Kurt to the companionway and down a steep ladder.

"In there." He slid open the door to the small cabin in the bow.

"Thanks. I'll be up in a minute."

There were two bunk beds on one side, a small sink and w.c. on the other. Below deck, it was definitely not a luxury boat, more like a working freighter. The salon was for show.

Alexis peered down the corridor. A heavy canvas curtain ran

down one side of the narrow passage. Behind it, a metal bulkhead
extended the length of the corridor. There appeared to be no opening. The yacht's secret must lie behind the bulkhead.

She made her way silently down to the stern, pushed aside
another curtain, and found a small galley—small refrigerator, mi-
crowave, shelf table, one chair. She crawled up on the table, leaned
over to the bulkhead which wasn't sealed at the top. She could just
see over. Behind the panels there was some kind of storage area.
She had to have a flashlight.

She sped down the corridor. In the cabin, she flushed the head,
removed one of her earrings, stuck it in her bra.

At that moment, Kurt leaned over the stairway, leering. "Hey,
the cabin's for later."

"I dropped an earring somewhere. They're my favorites. Do
you have a flashlight? I want to look for it."

He swore under his breath, tromped across the deck, then
thrust a large torch down the ladder. "Hurry up."

"I'll be right there."

Heart pounding, Alexis slipped back to the galley, quickly re-
mounted the table. The game would be up if he caught her here.

She shone the flashlight through the opening at the top of the
panels. Inside, steel mesh cages suspended from iron bars were
bolted to the hull. They looked like animal cages in a kennel,
except that the insides were tightly fitted with wooden crates. The
cages were designed to keep the crates from shifting when the boat
was underway.

The cargo obviously needed thorough protection. What was
it? Something precious, fragile. Certainly not heroine or hashish.

In an instant, Alexis knew. An archeologist picking up the
scent. She climbed down, took some deep breaths, quickly brushed
out her hair. She came back up to the main cabin smiling, wearing
both earrings.

Kurt was sprawled on the divan, working on his second beer.
He patted the seat beside him. When she sat down, he put his
hand on her thigh. She had to get out of there.

"Are you in Athens much?" she asked.

"Oh, a couple of times a year. Depends."

"On what?"

"Orders." His hand moved up her leg.

At just that moment, the radio came on at the bridge.

Kurt shouted, "Franz, get it."

When nothing happened, he roared, "*Scheisse*," and lurched toward the bridge.

Alexis grabbed her purse and shoes, ran for the gangplank. She raced to the end of the pier, the gravelly cement cutting her feet.

When he saw her coming, Theo started up the van. She jumped in, slammed the door, panting.

He swerved into the street. "I was about to come get you. You had me worried."

"Sorry, but it was worth it."

"You found out?"

"Not when and where, but what. The cargo area is filled with crates in iron cages bolted to the hull. They're definitely smuggling, and it's not narcotics."

"Guns?"

Alexis massaged her sore feet; she'd never get back into her shoes. "You're close—something breakable. From Greece."

He looked mystified. "What would foreigners want to take from Greece?"

"Nothing new, perhaps, but definitely a lot that's old. Antiquities—marbles, bronzes, icons."

"Panayiotis?"

"He's likely the middleman. He could never afford a boat like that. Someone else is in charge."

Theo said nothing for a long moment. "It makes sense. But antiquities? Now we're way in over our heads."

"We're not quitting now."

Up to then, Alexis had been haunted by the need to catch Panayiotis for their own sakes. If she were right about his precious cargo, it was now doubly urgent—for them and for Greece.

Her mind raced. The theft of Greece's national treasures incensed her, always had. Somehow, this nasty operation had to be checked. She thought she knew just the person to steer her onto the right track.

"Theo, this may be the one racket we *can* do something about."

CHAPTER 13

Alexis tensed, her neck and shoulders stiff, as she waited for Petros to answer the door. She'd decided to consult him in the heat of the moment. Now, she wondered if that had been a good idea.

She hadn't seen him since moving to Serros, hadn't spoken to him since she'd been released from jail. When she'd called last night, he'd sounded delighted. He'd finished surveying at the site in Messenia, was about to leave for Diana's villa. If he were still in high spirits, it'd be easier to talk to him.

"Alexi *mou, ti kaneis?*" Deeply tanned, black hair curling over the collar of his yellow polo shirt, wearing crisp white slacks, Petros looked like he belonged on the deck of a sloop.

Alexis felt disheveled in her rumpled khakis and faded tee shirt. Forget it, she told herself, and forget the past. This wasn't a social occasion. Petros was a professional, and she needed to pick his brain.

"You're not at your island hideaway?" he said.

She sought an easy subterfuge. "I had shopping to do. A coincidence you were in town."

"Sometimes the gods smile on us." He led her into the ultramodern living room, all leather, chrome, and glass, Diana's choice of decor. He motioned her to the beige leather sofa.

Alexis smiled nervously. "How'd it go at the dig?"

"Splendidly. The foundations of the *megaron* were more or less where I expected. We'll excavate next year." He sat down beside her. "You should come. We need volunteers. Only beautiful, and experienced, Americans need apply."

The same old charm, Alexis thought.

He flashed a grin. "How about you, Alexi? How are you doing since your little run-in with the law?"

"Five days in jail under suspicion of murder is hardly a little run-in."

"I won't remind you *who* argued against your moving to Serros." He was starting up again. She ignored his remark.

"Petros, I need to borrow some of your expertise."

"Why not?"

"I'd like you to keep this confidential. And no cross-examination."

"Sounds mysterious. My lips are sealed."

Was he going to cooperate? She took a deep breath. "A few weeks ago I learned the death of Loukas Koutsos was not murder. He died of natural causes, a heart attack. That's why I was released from jail."

"Oh, I didn't hear the details." He shifted around to face her. "If he died of a heart attack, what was his body doing in your olive orchard?"

"*His* orchard. It was an attempt to frame me for murder."

Petros arched his eyebrow. "The culprit?"

"The other Koutsos cousin, Panayiotis, along with Loukas' wife. They're the reason I'm here. They're smuggling. I need a short course from you on stolen antiquities."

"A peasant from Serros smuggling antiquities?"

"Didn't you tell me everyone and his brother is trading in antiquities? Panayiotis is no art expert, but he's moving stolen objects out of Greece. That's all I can tell you right now."

He sighed deeply. "Alexi, why don't you go on about your life? Panayiotis isn't going to bother you any longer."

"Not true. In fact, I have every reason to believe he still wants me out of the way." She tossed back her hair, twisted it into a knot. "Petros, I'm talking about Greek antiquities. You, of all people, should be concerned."

"I would be—if I thought there were a scrap of truth to your story. Do you have any proof?"

She sat mute.

"I thought not. Even if you did, why must *you* be the concerned citizen? Greece isn't even your country."

She'd heard this line—you can't understand because you're not Greek—before. It always rankled. More so, coming from him. "Does being born Greek guarantee concern about Greece's patrimony? I suppose, then, the illegal art dealers, smugglers, and corrupt officials in this country are all Armenian."

"I didn't say all Greeks are saints. I just meant—"

"I shouldn't get involved. That's not an option."

Petros reached for her arm. "Alexi, don't get upset. I'm trying to tell you something. Art theft is complicated—and dangerous."

She suppressed her irritation. "I need to understand those complications. Now. The only issue is whether or not you'll help me."

"Of course I'll help you. I'm only trying to protect you from yourself." He half-smiled, half-grimaced. "I'm going to make coffee. Let's sit outside. Make a list of your questions. I've got until noon."

"Thanks. Coffee would be great."

From the canopied veranda, Alexis looked out over Rigillis Street. With so many Athenians out of town, the air was fresh. The charm of Athens in summer was a well-kept secret.

What was so complicated about antiquities theft, she wondered. Where was the danger, except for getting caught? Art dealers didn't have shoot-outs or turf wars like drug pushers. Art theft was white collar crime. From what she'd read, everyone in the business—dealers, auction houses, collectors—seemed to be getting away with it.

Petros set a tray with Greek coffee and a bowl of grapes on the glass tabletop. "Ready?"

"Yes."

"Okay. Art theft is the world's third largest illegal activity after arms sales and narcotics—an estimated six to twelve billion dollars a year."

"Amazing. Anyone you know getting rich?"

"Probably, but nobody talks to me. What a boon government prohibition of the trade has been."

"Aren't people turning stuff in? I thought the Greek government pays people who find antiquities."

"Even if the government paid real money, which it doesn't, the illegal traders can make ten times as much on the black market."

"Why did you say art theft is complicated?"

"There's usually a long trail between the originator of the theft, let's say the finder, and the ultimate purchaser. The value of the object, as well as the difficulty of tracing it, increases with each transaction."

"By the finder, you mean the farmer or fisherman?"

"Or grave robber, looter, museum thief. These days some peasants spend all day in their fields with metal detectors. Still, the finder usually ends up with as little as one percent of the object's ultimate value."

"So the dealer cleans up?"

"Each person along the way takes a piece of the action. Different people do different tasks—storage, transportation, defacement of the object to hide its origins. The smugglers often cross national boundaries. Let's say Panayiotis *is* a smuggler and his role is getting the stuff out of Greece. After that, someone else takes over. The object may go into storage for years."

"Why?"

"To legalize ownership. For example, in Switzerland stolen objects stored in a bank for five years become the legal possession of the purchaser."

Alexis was incredulous. "The Swiss are facilitating the trade?"

"They're not alone. Most industrialized countries, the purchasing countries, have refused to sign international accords for the return of stolen art. Your country's the exception."

"Happy to hear it. Let's get back to the dealer. He arranges export and finds the buyer?"

"Generally."

"What kind of people are they, say, in Greece?"

"Since antiquities trading is illegal, they're usually people who have a lot of official contacts and cash to bribe museum guards, police, customs officials. These civil servants make so little money, it's easy to do."

"Then it's more who you know than how much you know about art."

Petros chortled. "The best dealers know both."

"Nobody knows who the dealers are?"

He tapped his fingers impatiently. "There are rumors—everyone in the art world has suspicions—but it's hard to identify them. It's not like the old days when Lord Elgin put into Piraeus, loaded up a ship, and simply sailed away."

"Somebody's loading up ships or trucks or planes. You said business is booming."

"True. Especially in eastern Europe and the Middle East. The great prizes used to be classical antiquities, but they've gotten scarce. Now they trade in just about anything, from Asia to Africa."

"But there's still a market for classical art."

Petros threw back his head and laughed. "If you find it, Alexi, I guarantee you'll sell it." He looked at his watch. "I know you don't like Diana's parties—"

"I must get back to Serros. My cats haven't seen me in days, and I've got to feed a neighbor's chickens while she's away."

Petros sized her up. "We've lost you to Serros."

"I wouldn't say that. I'm coming back to Lincoln in the fall. I'll be in Serros only on weekends."

"Why not make a complete return?" He reached for her hand, held it. "I've missed you."

Alexis gently withdrew her hand. "Let's not do this. I came to talk about stolen antiquities. You were a big help, and I appreciate it."

"Alexi, why not put the past behind us and start over?"

"It's too late. We've drifted too far apart."

"It's never too late." He caressed her cheek.

She saw he wasn't going to quit. "I'm trying to tell you there's someone else."

"Who?"

Alexis wasn't ready to go public. Certain Athenian friends would come unglued about Theo. She definitely didn't want to start re-entry with Petros. "*Who* is not the point."

He took her arm. "I insist you tell me. I have a right to know."

"A right?"

"What am I supposed to do? Go around Athens in the dark, everyone else knowing about your betrayal?"

"Betrayal? Our relationship was—is—over."

"Alexi, I insist on knowing. Duplicity does not become you."

Alexis felt the blood rushing to her face. He'd succeeded in provoking her as he doubtless knew he would. "If you must know, it's my stonemason, Theo."

"The Albanian?" He banged the glass table top.

"Before you attack him, I'm leaving."

"Why would I attack *him*? He's doing what every immigrant in his position would do—attach himself to a rich American."

"I can't believe you said that. He didn't attach himself to me, and I'm not rich."

"You are to him."

"This discussion is turning ugly. Theo and I care for each other. It's obviously a difficult situation, given the way people think."

"Difficult? It's absurd. Alexi, why are you going out of your way to alienate everyone in your life? You won't have a friend left."

"Not true. Helen and Yiannis have been very supportive. So has Aunt Georgia."

"Jesus Christ. I'm sorry I ever introduced you to that crazy woman." He rolled his eyes. "A stonemason."

Alexis sprang up, searched for her canvas bag. "This may sound strange to you, but Theo has more purpose in life than you'll ever have."

"Alexi, you're making me a joke. I can just hear people saying you left me for an Albanian."

She strode across the veranda. "Some people may say that. It's prejudice, pure and simple, a prejudice you seem to share. You're obviously more concerned about your hurt pride than anything or anyone else."

"You can call it prejudice. I call it common sense."

He lunged toward the front door, grabbed her bag from the floor in the hall, and shoved it at her. "Don't come running to me, Alexi, when this blows up in your face."

"Don't worry."

Alexis marched purposefully down the quiet street, wondering if Petros were watching from the veranda. Would he have behaved so badly if someone other than Theo—an American or another Greek—had come into her life? She doubted it. Was this the kind of attitude she'd have to confront from now on?

Never mind. There was no time to worry about any of it now. She'd gotten what she came for—some idea of who and what to look for. Panayiotis could well be in the antiquities game, a small fish in a big pond.

It was time to bait the hook.

CHAPTER 14

Alexis made her way to Vaso's apartment, fumbled in the gloom for her keys. A footstep on the landing made her jump. She spun around, caught sight of Theo down the hall. "You scared me. Have you been waiting long?"

A finger to his lips, Theo motioned for Alexis to open the door. She tugged him inside. "What's wrong?"

"I've been careless, Alexi. I followed Panayiotis back to his office this morning. He must have heard me. I dashed out the back, but he saw me. He tried to follow, but I lost him in the market." Theo slumped on the sofa, leaned back, his hand over his eyes.

"Never mind. He didn't catch you. What were you doing there anyway?"

"Trying to find out when the yacht sails. You're right. If we stay in Athens until it leaves, it'll be in and out of Serros before we catch up with it. I have an idea, but it will cost money."

"What?"

"I could ask my Albanian friends in Peristeri to cover the yacht. They look like types you see hanging around. As soon as the yacht sails, they could call me in Serros. We'd probably have six or eight hours."

"Remind me what the fisherman said about the deliveries."

"Vassilis said the yacht motors into the cove around two or three in the morning and anchors. Around six, the cabin cruiser shows up. They quickly move cargo from the cruiser to the yacht and both boats take off."

"So, if they keep to their usual schedule, the yacht would leave

Glyfada in the late evening to get to Serros by early morning. Maybe we should be watching the cruiser, too."

"We don't know where it's docked. It's not at the Dive Center. I checked. The yacht's our only possibility."

"Then let's call your friends."

"I should offer fifty dollars a day."

"Call them. I'll be in the kitchen."

*   *   *

Theo smiled as he pulled out the kitchen chair. "They'll be in Glyfada in an hour—with fishing poles."

Alexis gave him a hug. "I'm making a cheese omelet. Would you slice the bread?" Alexis served the omelet from the pan. "So. We return to Serros and get a phone call from your friends. Then what?"

"We bring in the Coast Guard."

"That's even harder than going to the police. The Greek Coast Guard will not come running when two foreigners, with no credibility and no proof, report a possible smuggling operation underway."

"Agreed. That's why we've got to get someone respectable to call them."

"Whom do you have in mind?"

"Petros Diamandopoulos, the well-known archeologist."

Alexis winced. "Petros won't help."

"Why not? What did he say when you told him about Panayiotis?"

"He didn't believe me, and we didn't end the meeting on good terms." She hesitated, decided to be open. "Petros was pushing to resume our relationship. I had to tell him no. He's not about to help me—us."

Theo seemed to be suppressing a smile. "We'll find someone else."

"Who?"

"Let's think about it. We need to get back to Serros."

"There's a ferry at four."

"I'll go with you."

"Is that wise? If Panayiotis knows you've been watching him, he could be laying a trap in Serros."

"I'm planning to lay low. I'll hide in the van until the ferry gets underway, get off with the passengers. I've told Vassilis I'm coming. I'll stay on his *kaiki*."

He carried his dishes to the sink. "Alexi, I'm more worried about you alone at the *liotrivi*."

"I've got to go home. I've got to feed the cats and Popi's chickens."

"Why don't you stay at Popi's? That way Panayiotis won't know you're back. You'll be safer."

"That's not a bad idea." Alexis yawned, suddenly very tired. "I need to lie down for a bit. Will you wake me in a half an hour?"

"I'll do better than that. I'll lie down with you and set my watch alarm."

She smiled. "Theo, was Hydra a dream? We were so relaxed." He kissed her, pulled down the light bedspread on Vaso's bed, and gently placed a pillow under her head. "Rest."

Alexis stared at the ceiling, her mind churning. What could they tell the Coast Guard? She hadn't actually seen stolen antiquities, only cargo containers. They could be for legitimate freight. No. No one would go to such lengths—crates inside steel cages, hidden behind a bulwark—for ordinary cargo. Still, the Coast Guard wouldn't act on mere speculation. Should she try Petros? He wouldn't even take her phone call. Maria and Nikos? No. She couldn't ask her lawyers to go out on a limb. In any event, Maria and Nikos were on vacation. They checked their office phone for messages, but how often?

Theo lay snoring lightly beside her. Worry about him nagged at her more than she'd let on. Panayiotis might not physically harm her, but an Albanian would be fair game.

Theo opened his eyes. "You're not sleeping."

"I don't see how we're going to pull this off."

"Alexi, I can stop the yacht."

"How?"

"I have an idea. I need to work out some things in Serros. Right now, we should contact Maria and Nikos, tell them what's going on."

"I had the same thought." She reached for the phone. "I'll start leaving messages. Then we'd better go. There may be a long line for the ferry."

"We shouldn't leave the building together."

"I'm parked on the side street. Why don't you take the car keys and leave from the rear entrance? I'll go out the front, stop at a kiosk for a newspaper. That will give you time to hide in the van."

* * *

Alexis watched the voluble Greeks sitting around her in the ferry's lounge, joking, complaining, arguing, flirting. She needed to think. Better to sit outside, even though the heat was intense. She found a deserted bench at the stern. Buddha-like, on crossed legs, she stared at the waves, then closed her eyes.

Her anger at Petros was deep. Stereotyping had come so easily—Theo, the preying immigrant; Alexis, the naive expatriate who would never find her way in Greece. Under Petros' charming veneer lay a cruel and egotistical character. She'd often blamed Diana for her son's weaknesses. Diana *had* been the sculptor, but the statue was now carved, had a cold, polished existence of its own.

Alexis buried her head in her arms. While Petros had been condescending and judgmental, his attitude toward immigrants was not that different from that of most of his countrymen. To be honest, if she were in America and involved with a black man or Latino, the attitude would be the same.

She was choosing a lonely and difficult life. Of course, there'd always be close friends who would support her and accept Theo, but they would be few. Most people would consider her an oddity—the American who was with the Albanian. Could she handle that?

Her thoughts turned to Panayiotis. Was Petros right? Was this a dangerous escapade? She reviewed her reasons for going after him. He was involved in a dirty game that offended her to the core. She couldn't forget he was after her, wanted to drive her from Serros. No, she had good cause.

How much villainy was Panayiotis capable of? Was killing animals just the surface? She'd told Theo that being spotted wasn't fatal, but they'd lost the element of surprise. Panayiotis knew they were watching him. He either had to get them out of his way or change his *modus operandi*.

Perhaps he wouldn't come to Serros now. He could load cargo at another island. That would be devastating. This was their chance to catch him, perhaps their one chance, and to empty those crates of their booty.

When Alexis caught sight of Serros in the hazy distance, she made her way down to the steamy car deck. No sign of Theo. She felt anxious, tried to function normally. Theo had a plan. She had to trust him. As the ferry ramp lowered to the pier, she spotted a blond head, but it was soon lost in the crowd.

*   *   *

The cats scampered toward Alexis when she unlocked the front door of the *liotrivi* late that afternoon. She scooped them up in her arms, their motors running at high speed.

Alexis surveyed her home with relief. The millstone, screw press, olive jars seemed like old friends. She was tempted to stay in the press that evening, but Theo was coming to Popi's. She packed a change of clothes and some food, put out food for the cats, picked up her instructions for feeding the chickens, and headed down the hill.

She encountered no one on the road. She hid her van in Popi's shed. Not wanting to alert the neighbors, she fixed a sandwich in the evening shadows from the bread and cheese she'd brought. It would be a long night if Theo didn't come soon.

She retrieved the cotton sheet folded at the end of Popi's bed, and stretched out on the roomy sofa in the living room. A screech owl whistled softly. The sleep that had eluded her earlier gently numbed her body, then her mind.

When her cell phone jarred her awake, Alexis wondered where she was until she recognized Popi's dowry chest. She grabbed the handset; the caller could only be Theo.

"*Ela.* Where are you?" she said. "What time is it?"

"Near midnight. Sorry I couldn't make it. I'll explain tomorrow. Did you hear from Maria?"

"No. I left another message, giving her the number for my cellular. Did you hear from Glyfada?"

"No. That means we have some time. I'll come out there tomorrow afternoon. Are you okay?"

"Yes. All's quiet. I fell into a deep sleep. I had a weird dream."

"Go back to sleep. Dream of me."

"Theo, can I reach you during the day?"

"No. Don't worry. I'll be at Popi's by five or six."

"Please be careful."

Alexis pulled the sheet up to her neck to take cover from a dive-bombing mosquito. What had she been dreaming about? The temple, but not her usual nightmare.

She'd been running up the hillside. Someone else was behind her, not chasing her, but trying to reach the temple before she did. It was a race she had to win.

She got up for a glass of water, sat perplexed at the kitchen table, the moonlight filtering in the window. They were still missing a basic piece of the puzzle.

She went over the facts one more time. Panayiotis wanted her out of Serros because he needed the *liotrivi*. Not for a warehouse; he could have a warehouse anywhere. For its location. At the foot of the hill, below the temple.

"It's possible," Alexis murmured.

If the wild idea running through her head didn't seem too crazy tomorrow, she'd have her work cut out for her.

CHAPTER 15

Pale gray light filtered through the rustling pine trees, just enough for Alexis to distinguish the narrow path up to the temple. She held off using her flashlight, not wanting to reveal her whereabouts. She should have waited until the sun rose over the mountain, but her half-dream impelled her to start out as soon as she woke.

The chill air was energizing. She'd driven from Popi's house to the olive press, sprinted up the mountainside, all in less than thirty minutes. No time to feel afraid. She squeezed her pack, feeling for the ball of cord Popi used for tying egg baskets. Today, she'd play Ariadne.

As dawn broke over the mountaintop, Alexis inspected the area around the little white church. There were signs of recent visitors—a plastic water bottle, cigarette butts, dirt that had been turned over, then smoothed out again. She circled the huge rectangular stones that formed the base of the ancient sanctuary. More butts, a crushed cigarette box, evidence of digging. What could Panayiotis have been doing up here?

She had to check out the cave. Not giving herself an opportunity to think twice, she scaled the boulders in front of the cliff and planted herself before the seam that marked the way in. She tied the cord around a lichen-covered boulder.

With the flashlight in one hand and ball of cord in the other, she threaded her way, step by step, through the narrow passage in the cliff. Her footsteps crunched on the pebbles. Several times, the cord caught on a piece of sandstone jutting out from the walls, making her jump. She breathed deeply, untangled the cord, giving it plenty of slack.

At the mouth, Alexis rotated her flashlight by degrees around the huge cavity. Thank God, the chamber was empty—no body wrapped in a sheet, no poisoned animals, claws clenched in agony. Slowly, she traversed the earthen floor to the back of the cave, still playing out the cord as she went. The skylights that had illuminated the shrine that day with Theo gave little natural light now. Too early. She shined her flashlight on the hollowed out formation, which gleamed.

Contemplating the goddess form, a calm enveloped her. She caressed the lustrous surface with her hand. It was a different material from the cave's sandstone interior—white streaked with brown, a rich vein of marble. Its shape—a cave within a cave—made the place palpably female.

Alexis threaded her way back to the main chamber, shining her light on the walls. Here and there, the stone had eroded, forming alcoves several feet high off the ground. Her pulse began to race again. She'd have to crawl through apertures in the rock.

Leaning into the first alcove, she projected her light inside. It was a small space, a perfect hiding place. The powdery dust on the ground seemed disturbed, but the alcove was empty. She moved on to the next opening, dropped to her knees. She couldn't see into the farthest recesses without entering. She took a deep breath and crawled through the hole. Something was there. Along the wall lay shards of pottery and stubs of candles. A storage chamber. One small, broken pitcher, probably used for pouring libations of oil or wine. She reached for it, then recalled her training about leaving artifacts in place.

The two other alcoves also showed traces of a human presence—bits of wood, an iron prong. Yet, nothing to confirm her suspicion Panayiotis was using the cave. Disappointed, she cast her light one last time around the main chamber. To her left lay a pile of rocks. Had there been anything on the ground when she and Theo had come? Alexis didn't think so. She shined her light on the rocks, decided to perform a small excavation. She rested the flashlight on a ledge and, starting from the edge of the pile, removed the rocks one by one, laying them in a line for reassembling.

Consumed with maintaining the original shape of the pile, Alexis didn't notice the piece of white stone until she touched it. Her heart pounding, she picked up the marble, took it over to the flashlight. Exquisite carving: soft folds, like cloth, a piece of drapery from an ancient robe or tunic. She ran her hand over the cool ripples of marble, felt a communion with the sculptor who'd shaped the stone thousands of years before.

She gently laid the marble on the ledge and returned to the rock pile, digging even more carefully. After removing another five or six stones, she gasped—a woman's arm. She held the marble to her breast. Was it Artemis, as Petros had hypothesized, or a mountain nymph that had frolicked on the pediment? Were her face, maidenly form, bow and arrow buried in the rock pile?

Alexis squatted on the ground, buried her head in her knees to clear her mind. How had the marbles come there? She felt certain of Panayiotis' involvement. Had someone discovered the marbles and sold them to Panayiotis?

It must have been around Easter, given his sudden interest in re-claiming the *liotrivi*. He'd stored the marbles in the cave while he found a dealer and arranged transportation out of Greece. The yacht would stop at Serros to take away the haul as soon as Panayiotis could get the marbles from the mountaintop to the cove. Alexis had most definitely been in the way.

She quickly replaced the rocks she'd removed, returning the first piece of marble to its hiding place. She'd take the limb with her, as proof of theft, just in case Panayiotis slipped through their hands. Unless . . . She might find something better. She took down her flashlight, shined it on the far side of the pile. A glimmer of white. Alexis tried not to rush in her excitement. She carefully moved stones aside to get at the piece of rounded marble covered by curlicues. She removed a head, face down, small enough to hold in the palm of her hand. She turned the head over, beamed light on the face—eyes wide open, nose short, slightly turned up mouth in a half-smile. Enchanting. Only one ear and part of the crown were missing.

"Artemis," she murmured. "Where have you been hiding?"

Alexis pulled off her sweatshirt, gently wrapped it around the head. She buried the marble in the bottom of her pack, replaced the marble limb in the pile, and picked up the ball of cord. At the passageway, she turned to take a last look at the chamber, to feel the power of the place.

Outside, the sunlight stunned her. She shielded her eyes, checked her watch. Eight o'clock. She'd been in the cave over an hour. She clutched her pack to her chest as she hurried down the path.

On the way back to Popi's, she'd stop at the *liotrivi*, hide the marble, call Maria again. Now that she had proof of Panayiotis' crimes—at least proof in her own mind—she had no qualms about involving Maria.

Where to hide the head? Not inside. Panayiotis would tear the press apart to find it. Outdoors would be better. She could bury it in one of the geranium pots, even better, put it in one of the huge clay oil jars she'd weighted down with olive pits. The necks were just wide enough to insert the head. No, too obvious, the first place a Greek would look.

As she approached the *liotrivi*, it hit her. She'd hide the head on Loukas' land in the stump of a burned olive tree. Poetic justice. She found a large tree trunk close to the house, cleared out a place in the charred wood, laid her treasure in the hole, covered it with dirt and ashes. Pleased with her hiding place, she went inside to check her cell phone for messages.

"Alexi, this is Maria calling. We are in Corinth. The number is 0741 17652."

Alexis let out a whoop, punched in the numbers. "May I speak with Maria Antonides, please? This is Alexis Davidov."

After what seemed a very long time, Maria's breathless voice came on the line. "Sorry, I was in the garden. We're at my in-laws' house."

"Maria, so much has happened, is happening. We're on the verge of trapping Panayiotis."

"Who's we?"

"Theo and I are in Serros."

"Alexi, you're not supposed to be with Theo."

"It's my call. I needed help. He's the only one."

Silence from Maria.

Alexis launched into her story of snooping round the yacht, discovering the crates. "Maria, I know what those crates are for. Antiquities. We've got to bring in the Coast Guard."

"And tell them what? There are crates on a yacht? We don't *know* they're transporting antiquities."

Alexis laughed. "We do now. I just came from the temple, actually from the cave behind it. Maria, I found marbles—pieces of an ancient statue. Panayiotis is smuggling them out of Greece. That's why he had to have the *liotrivi*."

"Slow down, *pedi mou*. You found marbles?"

"Yes, I didn't stay long enough to examine the whole cache, but I brought one marble head, a lovely thing, with me as proof."

"Alexi, you're in possession of a stolen object. That's serious. You must turn it over immediately, report what you found."

"Reporting might save the marbles, but it won't stop Panayiotis. We've got to catch him in the act. Theo's working on that, but we need you to alert the Coast Guard."

"Listen, we'll catch Panayiotis some other way. The best thing is to go right now to the authorities with your marble head."

"Maria, he's almost in our grasp. Look, stand by. I'll get more proof."

"I can tell you're determined. Please be careful. I'll talk to Nikos. Maybe we can figure out a strategy. Get back to me soon."

"I will. Very soon."

Alexis drove to Popi's, parked the van in the shed. The chickens came next. She let herself into the smelly coop, filled the troughs with fresh water from the hose, spread the feed in pans around the yard. The chickens fanned out toward the pans, squawking. Basket on her arm, she collected eggs from the nests. Sweating from her morning's exertions, Alexis collapsed on the sofa in Popi's darkened front room. She prayed Theo would get there by early afternoon. Until then, she'd try to contain her excitement.

*   *   *

Alexis woke from her nap feeling apprehensive. No word from Theo. She showered, changed into a clean shirt and shorts. Ravenous, she searched Popi's pantry for spices, concentrated on making a spaghetti sauce. She hoped Theo would show up by the time she had a meal ready.

A car rumbled past. Otherwise, it was dead quiet with most of the village down at the harbor for a local Serros festival.

Alexis stayed with her decision not to turn on lights. She took her chopping board over to the window sill to work in the fading daylight. The pungent smell of onions and garlic sauteing in the skillet reminded her she hadn't eaten since her breakfast on the run.

As Alexis worked, she considered taking Theo to bed in Popi's room. Popi wouldn't mind, but Thanos would. He wouldn't have to know. Alexis stared at the cutting board, not seeing the peppers she was chopping. She was back in Hydra, caressing Theo's hard chest and broad shoulders, feeling his pleasure-giving hands move over her body.

Over the hissing pan, she heard something outside. Excitedly she lowered the flame, hurried out to the front room, tugged open the door.

"What have we here?" Panayiotis charged in, grabbed Alexis by the arm and slammed the door behind him.

He thrust her against the heavy wood dining table.

She circled it, out of his reach. "Get out of here. This is Popi's house."

"I know damn well whose house it is. Where's the Albanian?"

"What Albanian?"

"I'm not playing games, bitch. Where is he?"

"I have no idea. He left here after Easter."

Panayiotis yanked the light cord over the table. Alexis recoiled from the brightness. When she looked back at Panayiotis, he had a pistol trained on her.

The gun made her angry. "I'm taking care of this house. I don't know what the hell you're doing here, but if you don't leave immediately, I'll report you for breaking in."

"Breaking in? A visit to my old classmate?" He chortled.

"What exactly do you want?"

"Exactly, I want you and the Albanian, but you'll do. We'll get him later." He looked around, sniffed the air.

"I've got food cooking," she said. "I've got to turn off the stove."

He pointed the gun toward the kitchen. "Don't try anything."

As if she could with him waving a gun at her. Her only weapon was her wits. She left the food out. Theo would at least know she'd been there, waiting for him.

"Now get your stuff. We're going for a ride. Give me your keys."

As Alexis gathered her pack from the sofa, she slid out her phone and wallet with Maria's number. She prayed Theo would find them, get the message. Panayiotis herded her out the front door, leaving the house unlocked.

Dusk. Alexis did some quick calculations. Too dark to go to the temple. Panayiotis must have already moved the marbles. His car must be parked at his house on the other side of the village. If the operation was on for tonight, he was probably heading to the cove.

Where was Theo? Why hadn't he come out to Pygi? Her only hope was he'd learned from his friends in Piraeus that the yacht had sailed and he'd get to the cove in time.

Panayiotis marched her over to the van, yanked open the door on the driver's side. "You're driving. My house." He kept the pistol on Alexis as she drove. "Pull up over there."

The blue truck from the dive center was parked next to Panayiotis' small stucco house. Two men came out. Alexis recognized them from the yacht, the thin one by his goatee, the hefty one by his red baseball cap.

"Tie her hands," Panayiotis ordered. He sneered at Alexis. "Get out."

Alexis felt her nerve failing. Three to one. Tied up, she'd be helpless. She took a last stab. "Up to now, Panayioti, you were a common criminal. This is kidnapping. The worse you make it for me, the worse for you when you're caught."

The young man with the goatee, concern on his face, looked at Panayiotis.

"You're proposing I let you go?" Panayiotis shook his head in disgust. "Tie her. Then load up."

The two men bound her wrists with rope, then lugged cartons from the house to the back of the van. Alexis counted five, enough for the marble pieces from the temple.

"Put her on the floor in the back," Panayiotis ordered. "Tie her hands to the braces under the seat."

Alexis took a deep breath. "That's not necessary."

"Shut up."

The men picked Alexis up under the arms, dropped her on her back across the floor of the van, and knotted the rope, binding her hands to the iron brace under the seat.

Alexis barely heard Panayiotis mutter, "Now take the truck and find the Albanian. He's got to be somewhere in town. We'll meet at the boat."

Thank God. They didn't have Theo, didn't know where he was. Panayiotis seemed to be improvising. Theo had been working up a plan. All she had to do was stay cool. She kept telling herself that, tried to believe it.

Panayiotis started up the van, soon veered off the road. The van lurched on rough track through the forest. When it finally stopped, Alexis was sore from the jostling, desperate to know where they were.

"Listen, I've got to get out. I need a bathroom."

"A bathroom," Panayiotis mimicked. "I thought you were a country girl."

He snorted, got out, and came around. "Go squat on the beach. You make one move to run, and I'll shoot you—gladly."

He untied her, held the pistol on her as she slid out of the van. They were at the cove. Scorched pine trees stood forlornly on the shore. Charred wood, looking like the remains of a shipwreck, littered the beach. A band of white from the rising moon glimmered over the sea, lighting the narrow neck of the cove.

When Alexis returned to the van, Panayiotis motioned her to a rock across from him. He lit a cigarette. "You were lucky in court. You should still be in jail."

"This isn't much better."

"Who knows what's to come?" He laughed, enjoying his bit of sadistic humor.

"If anything happens to me, they'll come looking for you. My lawyers know I'm in Serros, tracking you. I've made sure of that."

"I'll be long gone. No trail whatsoever. And you?" He grunted. "I've heard moonlight swims can be dangerous. People drown."

Alexis thought he was bluffing but couldn't be sure. Don't react, she told herself, just get through the next few hours.

He smirked, tossed his cigarette butt on the beach. "How are your cats? How many have you got left?"

Alexis stared for a moment, then, exploding in rage, charged him. His pistol glanced off the side of her head. She staggered back, hit the rock, and fell to the ground.

Panayiotis glowered. "That was stupid. Get in the van." He prodded her with the gun toward the van, roughly pushed her down, and roped her wrists tightly to the brace.

*   *   *

Pain surged through Alexis' neck and back. She'd lain in the same excruciating position for several hours.

She heard a low rumble, followed by the hum of a motorized

anchor chain. The yacht had arrived. Next, a low horsepower motor, probably the dinghy coming in to shore.

The back door of the van swung open. "Move these cartons to the yacht," Panayiotis said to his men, "very carefully. When you're done, come back for the girl."

They were taking her on board. Would they wait for the cabin cruiser to show up with additional cargo? Maybe they'd leave right away, taking only the marbles from the temple.

Theo couldn't know that. She had to stall, keep her captors from leaving. She could think of only one bluff.

Panayiotis thrust open the side door. "Ready for a little cruise? I hear you like yacht parties." He smirked, cut the rope to the brace, rolled her over. "Your friend Kurt's waiting for you."

Alexis tried not to show surprise. How'd he know about her visit to the yacht? Kurt must have told him about Lisa; Panayiotis caught on quickly. Well, it didn't change anything now.

Panayiotis yanked her by the arm toward the black rubber boat on the shore. "Get in." He climbed in behind her.

The guy in the baseball cap steered toward the *Frederika*, the huge boat motionless, seemingly deserted, a phantom in the moonlight. He pulled alongside the ladder, shut off the motor.

Panayiotis pointed at Alexis. "Move."

"I can't possibly climb that ladder with my hands tied."

"You are a pain in the ass." He pulled out a pocket knife, cut the rope, then took the pistol out of his jacket pocket. "You try anything, we solve the problem of one nosy foreigner."

Her hands free, Alexis felt less vulnerable. "You solve your problem with a gun, we both lose. Lots of people know what you're up to. I'd be sorry to miss your murder trial."

"Up the ladder, bitch."

CHAPTER 16

Alexis peered through the porthole, desperately watching for the first hint of dawn. Kurt had shoved her down the hatch and locked her in the small cabin as soon as she and Panayiotis boarded. She'd had no chance to try to delay the yacht's departure.

The smell of gasoline made her queasy; the lack of food and sleep, weak. She drank handfuls of water from the tap to prevent dehydration. In the dark, a droning mosquito inflicted torture, refusing to fly out the narrow opening of the porthole.

Alexis felt her body tensing. She lay down on the bunk to forestall a muscle spasm. Until now, she'd kept herself almost convinced she'd be rescued. A fairy tale. Real life didn't work that way.

Face the facts: there was no Theo, no Coast Guard rushing to save her. No *deus ex machina* would descend. The only way she'd get out of this would be by outsmarting them.

The question crept in, despite all her efforts to keep it at bay. Would Panayiotis kill her? Until he struck her on the beach, he'd avoided violence—except against innocent animals. There was a reason for that. Violence was costly. He could get away with a lot as long as he stuck to property crime.

Her breathing quickened. She'd go with what she'd planned, make the story even stronger.

At last, footsteps overhead, then the hatch cover thumping onto the floor of the salon. She pressed her ear to the cabin door, straining to hear. Several men lumbered down the ladder, seemed to gather at the far end of the gangway.

Alexis banged on the door. "Let's talk," she yelled. "I'm ready to make a deal."

Heavy footfalls. The outside bolt scraped against wood, the cabin door flew open.

Kurt's massive frame blocked the doorway. "So the party girl wants to deal."

Alexis steeled herself. "You've got a pretty good haul this trip. Who'd have thought there'd be marbles in Serros? Too bad you can't sell the entire lot."

"Oh no?"

"Headless statues don't go for much, unless it's the Venus de Milo." Alexis feigned supreme confidence.

Panayiotis pushed forward. "What do you know about the marbles?"

"I've been exploring the cave ever since I arrived in Serros."

Panayiotis ran his fingers through his hair, evidently confused.

Now, she told herself, now. "It's an excellent antiquities market these days. I'm sure the bodies will get you something, but think how much more you'd get with the whole statue. Marble heads are priceless."

"What heads?"

"The ones I took from the rock pile in the cave. Yesterday, in the early morning."

"You did what?"

"They were charming heads—smiling, faces like goddesses."

"Christ."

Kurt clasped Alexis' neck in his hand, turned her head toward him. "You're the best liar I've ever seen. I don't believe this crap."

"If I'm lying, you'll find the heads in the cartons," she said, twisting out of his grasp. "If not, I'm the only one who can tell you where they are."

"Bullshit." He pushed her back into the cabin and bolted the door.

Moments later, Alexis heard shouting, an argument on the main deck. She'd planted seeds of doubt. If only they'd start unpacking the cartons to search. At least one head was missing;

she prayed it would appear two were gone. She lay down to consider her next move.

*   *   *

The *Frederika* rocked gently. Alexis pressed against the porthole. The cabin cruiser, barely visible in the dark gray light, glided past at low speed, turned, and anchored on the port side. Time had run out. The yacht would take off as soon as the additional cargo was brought on board.

She listened to the crew moving around on the deck, a groaning noise followed by a thud. The yacht's gangplank had been lowered to the cruiser. Feet tramped through the salon, crossed to the hatch.

The hatch opened. Grunts, swearing in Greek and German. Was cargo being moved up or down? The heavy metal bulkhead slid open. Was the crew removing the cartons from behind the bulkhead to examine them?

"Now bring that bitch," Panayiotis shouted.

The cabin door opened and the guy with the goatee told to Alexis to follow him. He looked uncomfortable, didn't manhandle her.

At the top of the ladder, she found the entire company in the salon—Panayiotis and the hefty guy in the red cap, Kurt and Franz, two swarthy strangers in light anoraks, apparently from the cabin cruiser.

"Wouldn't want the party girl to miss the party," Kurt said, kicking one of the cartons out of his way.

Panayiotis motioned to his men. "Unpack them."

The cartons were stuffed with straw. Inside were large objects, wrapped in cloth like a horse blanket, bound with thick rope. They removed them, one by one, from the cartons, laid them on the floor. They looked from Panayiotis to Kurt, seemingly unsure who was giving the orders.

"What the hell," Kurt said. "We've wasted so much time already."

The two slit the ropes with knives, unwrapped the cloth. Despite her anxiety, Alexis was enthralled by the sight. At least twenty skillfully carved marble fragments lay sprawled on the turquoise carpet—arms, thighs, part of a girdle, hands, a sandal. No heads. Her gamble might pay off. "Two lovely females, probably Artemis and a nymph. Complete, they'd fetch millions of dollars," she chided. "How much of that would *you* get, Panayioti? Several hundred thousand?"

She was on dangerous ground now—they'd want the missing pieces badly. "Frankly, I don't give a damn about the marbles. They'll probably end up in my country anyway. It's time we made a deal."

Panayiotis narrowed his eyes. "What kind of a deal?"

"I have what you want. You have what I want. We trade."

"Trade what?"

"I give you the two missing heads in exchange for your and Loukas' properties." She silently blessed Georgia for the inspiration. "You come out way ahead on this one."

He glowered. "I can't sell you his land."

"You can get Nitsa to sell it, for next to nothing, of course."

"I need the heads now."

"You get one. I'll keep the other until you bring me the signed contracts for the land."

"Where's the head?"

"I'll take you to it."

"You're not going anywhere," Kurt growled.

Panayiotis turned on him angrily. "Are you crazy? We've got to get the rest."

Alexis fanned the flames. "In two hours, you'll be out of here with at least one complete statue."

"Two hours?" Kurt shouted. "No way. It's daylight. We've got to leave now."

"With what? Half a statue?" Panayiotis sneered. "I'm going for the head." He shook Alexis. "Where is it?"

She ignored his pressure on her arms. "We have a deal? You

release me when you get back to the yacht. You bring me the contracts within three days."

"And you turn over the other head."

"After my lawyer checks the contracts."

He nodded angrily.

"Okay. The first head. It's a pleasant work, a nymph, but nothing like the Artemis you'll get later. Once you get the nymph out, the goddess will be worth five times as much." A total bluff; Alexis was banking on his ignorance. "Go to Loukas' property. There's a large burned olive tree more or less in line with my kitchen window." Did he catch the irony? "In the trunk, under some soil and ashes, is the first head. Don't bother looking for the other one. It's nowhere around there."

"I'll be back in an hour, maybe a little more," Panayiotis told Kurt. "You wait. That's an order."

"Fuck your orders. If you're not back in ninety minutes, I sail."

Kurt shut Alexis in the cabin again. She'd gained time, but there was still no sign of Theo. Where was he? Pygi? In that case, he might catch Panayiotis on his way to the olive press, but the yacht would sail.

Kurt could put her ashore or leave with her on board. Still furious about the party deception, he'd probably dump her at sea—unless he was greedy enough to want the other, non-existent, head.

She shuddered.

*   *   *

Alexis felt certain an hour had passed. She could now see the shore clearly in the pink morning light. Six-thirty, seven. Watching out the narrow opening of the porthole, she searched for signs of movement on shore. Nothing.

She heard the distant chugging of a motor, craned her neck as far as she could, caught sight of something. Damn. Only a fisherman heading back to port.

Another motor, closer. The black rubber boat raced back from the shore. Was that Panayiotis stomping on board? He must have found the head. She'd gained time, but at what cost? She no longer had proof of his theft. She'd played her one card for nothing in return. At least, her captors didn't know that.

The anchor chain jangled at the bow, followed by the buzz of the motorized anchor. The yacht's engines caught. They were leaving.

Suddenly, everything stopped. The yacht fell strangely quiet, as if drifting. Alexis scrambled back to the porthole.

Two more fishing boats passed by. No, three. They weren't passing at all; they were tying up bow to stern across the neck of the cove. Two other *kaikis* appeared, joined the line.

Alexis caught on. "Thank God."

The hatch cover dropped with a thud. Heavy steps pounded down the passage. Kurt yanked the cabin door open. "Up on deck. You get a front row seat."

At the bridge, he ordered her into the captain's chair, tied her arms to the metal perch, and left. Six *kaikis*, gaily colored in blues, reds and yellows, stretched across the narrow neck of the cove. Alexis had the brief thought they'd make a lovely painting.

She heard yelling outside the bridge.

"The girl comes with me," Panayiotis screamed.

She swiveled around, caught sight of Panayiotis clutching a burlap bag to his chest.

"Don't be stupid," Kurt shouted back. "I need her to get past those damn boats. I go out with her on deck, a gun to her head."

"And me?" Panayiotis screamed.

"You follow in the cabin cruiser."

"No."

Kurt punched Panayiotis in the jaw, ripped the bag out of his arms. "Get off this boat before I throw you off."

Panayiotis swung at Kurt. The Greek was no problem for the huge German who landed another blow, now to his shoulder. Panayiotis struggled to stay on his feet. The man with the goatee rushed over to help him.

Kurt drew a revolver from his windbreaker. "Enough of this," he roared. "Get off before I kill you—all of you."

The Greeks disappeared from view. Alexis heard the gangplank come up. It was down to her and the two Germans.

The door to the bridge flew open. Kurt's face was blood red. "What are those idiots in the fishing boats up to?"

"I'd guess they're trying to stop you."

Kurt barked instructions at Franz in German. "We'll rope her to a cleat on the bow. Then you take the wheel. Leave the fishermen to me."

Kurt marched Alexis forward, kept his gun on her as Franz forced her down. Behind them, the cabin cruiser fired its engines. It took off, heading not toward the blocked cove entrance, but back toward shore.

A hoarse laugh broke from Kurt's throat. "Stupid thing to do. Good luck, Panayiotis."

The cabin cruiser ran aground. Alexis watched Panayiotis and the others jump off and scurry up the rocky beach. Suddenly, a shot rang out, then another. Five or six shouting men rushed out of the pine trees as Panayiotis and his men scattered in different directions.

Alexis wanted to cheer. She searched the shore for a blond head, then turned back to the *kaikis*. Where was Theo in all this? The fishermens' maneuver looked like something he'd think up, but he was nowhere to be seen.

Kurt stomped back to the bridge, seemingly ready to force his way out. Alexis tensed. When the fishermen saw their boats would be damaged, they'd break ranks, let the yacht through. Kurt got within twenty yards of the *kaikis*, idled, called Franz to take the wheel.

"Who's in charge of this show?" he shouted from the bow.

"The fishermen of Serros," a voice called out.

Alexis barely suppressed a grin. Her situation might be precarious, but she had the fishermen of Serros defending her. Theo must be there somewhere.

"Who speaks for them?"

A skinny young man, long hair pulled back in a pony tail, in a denim jacket and jeans, stepped out of the cabin on the middle boat. He puffed out his scrawny chest. "Vassilis."

"What the hell are you doing?" Kurt yelled.

"You have no eyes?"

"I can bust through this line any time, wreck one or two of your boats."

"So do it."

"Go to the devil. What do you want?"

"Everything you've got on board, including the American."

"You can have the woman. Forget the cargo." Kurt put his leg up on the railing, leaned on his knee. "It'd be a shame to destroy your boat. New *kaikis* cost a lot."

"Every fisherman here has a rifle. You try to run this line, you'll regret it."

"Don't be stupid. You think this boat is unarmed?"

Vassilis glared, put his hands on his hips. "Then it's a stand-off." He climbed back into the hold.

Kurt kicked a coil of rope. "*Scheisse.*"

Alexis had been thinking fast. If she could talk to Theo, maybe they could end the confrontation without violence.

"A shoot-out is stupid," she said to Kurt towering above her. "Give them the Serros marbles. That's what they really care about."

"These guys think they're heroes."

"Let me talk to them."

He looked away, gripped the railing. "Make it fast. Five minutes, and I'm out of here."

"I can't do this tied up."

Without a word, he untied the rope, pulled her up and back to the bridge. He revved his engine as he angled his bow between the two boats in the middle of the line, then switched on the loudspeaker. "Hey, fisherman. Someone wants to talk to you."

Alexis took the mike. "This is Alexi. Is Theo there?"

Theo immediately appeared on deck of the closest *kaiki*, waving his arms.

"Theo, can you and Vassilis come on board?"

"Come alongside," Theo called.

On a signal from Kurt, Franz swung the yacht parallel to the *kaiki*. Theo and Vassilis jumped on the deck.

"Inside." Kurt pointed with his gun toward the salon, then yelled to Franz. "Put it in idle. We get underway as soon as I say so."

Alexis stepped into the salon from the bridge, sat on one of the lounges. Seeing Theo so close, she felt a surge of relief. Theo nodded, his eyes twitching in a half-wink, as he sat across from her, Vassilis beside him.

Kurt leaned against the cabin door, his gun trained on them. "You've got exactly five minutes. What do you want?"

Theo leaned back, crossed his arms. "We don't know who you are, where you're from, or where you're going. But your friend, Panayiotis, tells us you've got antiquities on board. That means you're not going anywhere."

"Big words. Now I do know who you are, Albanian. You seem to forget you're on *my* boat and I've got *your* girlfriend."

"You seem to forget you're surrounded."

Alexis waved her hands. "We're supposed to be talking. Theo, what do you want to call off the fishermen?"

"We told him. You come with us and he unloads his cargo."

Kurt flushed bright red again. "This is crap."

Alexis saw he was close to exploding. "Wait a minute, dammit. Tell them what *you* want."

"I want these assholes out of the way in three minutes. You with them."

"Okay. A compromise. We leave with only the Serros marbles. You leave with the rest."

"Sure. You get the fucking statue, and I make a run for it with a bunch of church icons. Forget it."

"The fishermen won't let you take the marbles."

"Then, no deal." He waved the gun at Theo and Vassilis. "Get off. One passenger's enough."

Theo stood, pulled Alexis up. "She comes with us."

"Bah." Kurt jerked his head in refusal.

Theo stood his ground. "If you let her go, we'll let you out."

"No." "No, Theo." Alexis and Vassilis shouted together.

Giving up the marbles after all they'd been through? She snatched the burlap bag from the table.

Kurt ripped it out of her hands. "You get this stupid rock when I'm on my way. I'll hand it over at midships."

Alexis looked at Theo, who nodded. He tugged her through the cabin door and over the railing onto the gunwale of the *kaiki*.

Seconds later, safe in the *kaiki's* hold, Theo grabbed Alexis and held her to him. He touched the bruise on the side of her head.

"Panayiotis has a temper." She dropped her head onto his shoulder, breathing deeply to control her emotions. "If those guys weren't so greedy, they'd have left a lot earlier."

"Why didn't they? They're usually gone by dawn."

"I sent Panayiotis back to the *liotrivi* for the head. The one in the bag. I figured it would gain time."

"Smart, Alexi. We had a hard time convincing the fishermen to do this. We got the last one only this morning when he came back from fishing."

"Panayiotis?" she said.

Theo grinned. "That was your friend Michalis shooting. He radioed he got Panayiotis in the leg, then handed him over to the police."

They heard Vassilis on the prow shouting instructions to the other fishermen, who untied their boats and steered them apart just enough to make way for the yacht. Kurt barreled through the opening, scraping the *kaiki's* bow.

Alexis scrambled up to the deck. "Vassili, the head?"

Grinning, he dangled the burlap bag.

Alexis grabbed it to check the contents. "Thank God. One piece of evidence."

The *kaiki* rolled in the yacht's wake. Alexis, clutching Theo's arm, shook her head in dismay. "It kills me to see him get away."

"Not a chance. In less than five minutes he'll be boarded by the Coast Guard."

"Are you serious?"

He nodded. "As soon as I found your wallet at Popi's, I called Maria. When Maria understood it was kidnapping, she swung into action. We've been cooperating with the Coast Guard since early this morning."

"Where are they?"

"They couldn't stop the yacht until we confirmed you were on board. We radioed the Coast Guard as soon as we saw you tied up on deck." He laughed. "They're waiting for the yacht around the point."

Alexis hugged Theo ecstatically. "Is the Coast Guard boat fast enough?"

"Girl, it's a frigate," Vassilis said as he pointed his boat back to Serros harbor.

Alexis clapped Vassilis on the shoulder. "You fishermen should be very proud. When you see the marbles, you'll understand. They'll make Serros famous."

He shrugged. "Not too famous, I hope. Anyway, they'd have gotten away—the smugglers *and* the marbles—if not for Theo." They chugged back to the harbor, followed, like ducklings, by the five other boats. The bright sun on the water hurt Alexis' eyes. She stretched out on a thwart, her head on Theo's lap, but couldn't sleep. She shielded her eyes, squinted up at him. "We caught the small fry, but we still haven't hooked the big fish."

He looked surprised. "Who?"

"The dealer, the mastermind who set this up."

"The police will get that from Panayiotis," Theo said, stroking her hair.

"Most likely, he doesn't know. If what Petros told me is true, the dealer is many transactions away from the actual smugglers."

"Then there's no way for *us* to find him."

"Except we have something he desperately wants. When he discovers the Serros marbles are in the hands of the authorities, he'll be very disappointed. If he then finds out the best piece is still available—"

"Alexi, you've got to turn over that head as soon as we get back. Maria insisted."

"I still need it. I've got to trace the source of this deal. Otherwise, the smuggling will go on and on." She sat up, murmured in his ear. "I'm going to Athens for a couple of days. Are you with me?"

He frowned. "I should be thinking of Olga and my family."

"If we find the dealer, you'll be a national hero."

"Not interested. I want only to keep a very persistent woman out of trouble."

How things had changed. In jail, Alexis had protected Theo. Now, he'd stepped into the role of protector. She liked it. There was a mutuality, a parity, in their relationship she'd never known before.

Theo sat quietly, but she sensed the wheels turning. Finally, he said, "When are you going to tell me your plan?"

"*Our* plan. On the hydrofoil to Athens."

"The sooner we finish this business, the better."

She grinned in delight. "But you do want to finish it."

ATHENS

CHAPTER 17

Seeing Alexis and Theo at her door Sunday morning, Nitsa clutched the handle, then threw her weight against the door to close it. Theo wedged his foot in the doorway. Her hair a tangled mess, black mascara smeared under her eyes, Nitsa growled, "How dare you come here?"

"Don't play the victim, Nitsa," Alexis said angrily. "You and Panayiotis started this. If anyone has a right to be angry, it's me."

"You'd better listen," Theo said. "Right now, Panayiotis is under arrest for smuggling antiquities. He's done far more than that in the last twenty-four hours, doubtless with your help. You two could spend the rest of your lives in jail."

Nitsa stared at them through the crack in the door. "I don't believe you."

"You'd better believe it. The Coast Guard captured the yacht. Panayiotis is in prison." As planned, Theo switched to good guy mode. "Nitsa, we want information. If you provide it, they may not prosecute you. It could help Panayiotis. It's the only chance you've got."

Her eyes darted from one to the other, but she said nothing.

"I wonder what Panayiotis will do when he hears you refused to help him," Alexis said.

Nitsa whimpered. Then, clutching her pink frilly housecoat around her as if to protect herself, she stepped away from the door. Theo grabbed Alexis' arm, pulled her into the house.

Slippers flapping, Nitsa shuffled to the living room where she had covered every available surface with silk flower arrangements. She collapsed into a bamboo armchair. "What do you want from me?"

Theo stood before her, his expression grim. "Panayiotis kidnapped Alexis at gunpoint. Kidnapped. That's a very serious crime."

Nitsa shot an angry look at Alexis. "You weren't supposed to be there. You should never have bought the *liotrivi*."

"Even if I hadn't been there, you two were stealing antiquities from Greece."

Nitsa clammed up.

"Perhaps you were only in on the small stuff, the stuff you stored in the warehouse behind your store."

She threw back her head, stared at the ceiling. "How do you know about that?"

Theo turned to Alexis, put his finger to his mouth, looked back at Nitsa. "We have enough to put you and Panayiotis away for years. It's your choice: tell us what we need to know now, or go to prison."

She stared at him, mute.

He picked up the phone on the desk and asked for the police.

Nitsa groaned. "Stop this torture." She sighed heavily. "What do you want to know?"

Alexis slid in on cue. "Names. If your information's good, we won't bring you into the picture. If not—"

"What names?"

"The dealer you're working with. Who set all this up?"

"I can't tell you." Her voice quavered. "I don't know."

"Nitsa, let's not play games."

"I'm not," she cried. "They never tell you their names. We got instructions by phone. The money went directly into our bank account."

"What about pick-ups and deliveries?" Alexis persisted.

"We picked up at a warehouse in Drapetsona. The deliveries went to the yacht or the Dive Center."

Her responses flowed too easily. Alexis sensed she was hiding something. "What about the deliveries to Athens?"

Nitsa threw down her hands, palms up, as if to ask what else they could want. "It was only once or twice. I don't have a name, only an address."

"You will write down the address and any phone numbers you used. Also the address of the warehouse."

Nitsa shuffled over to a desk, opened a drawer, wrote on a scrap of paper. Hand trembling, she passed the paper to Theo. "That's the address in Athens. Only Panayiotis has the phone number. The other address is for the warehouse." She stiffened, tossed back her blond tangles. "Now get out of my house."

Theo put the paper in his shirt pocket. "With pleasure."

Alexis followed him to the door, turned back for a moment. "Don't try to tip anyone off, Nitsa. If anything happens to us, my lawyers go straight to the police."

* * *

They found a taxi easily on the empty, sun-baked streets. As they sped into Athens, Alexis asked to see the paper. She wrinkled her brow. "It's not possible."

"What?"

"This is the building where Diana Diamandopoulos lives."

Theo took her hand. "A coincidence. Petros' mother couldn't be an antiquities dealer."

Alexis fixed her gaze out the window, her mind racing. "She's a decorator. Maybe that's why Petros was so quick to discredit what I told him about Panayiotis. Maybe—"

"Alexi, there must be many apartments in that building."

"Actually, no. It's an old neo-classical mansion with only two floors, two apartments on each floor."

"Who lives in the other apartments?"

Alexis had a vague recollection of once meeting one of Diana's neighbors. Where? She stewed, wondering if Diana and Petros were implicated. Diana certainly had the money; Petros, the expertise.

As if reading her mind, Theo said, "We can't accuse anyone unless we know for sure. We'll get Nitsa to tell us which apartment."

"She's taken cover by now, but there's another way. I bet Georgia knows everyone in the building. She's family, remember?"

As soon as they got back to Vaso's, where Alexis was staying, they phoned Georgia in Sounion. The maid said Mrs. Diamandopoulos had gone for a swim, would be back for her afternoon nap. They left a message.

Alexis' stomach churned. She shouldn't rush to judgment. Diana could have gotten into it innocently. Petros might be many things, but he wasn't a criminal. Still, the antiquities were delivered to Diana's building.

Theo broke into her train of thought. "We could do with some food."

"I don't think there's much in the house."

"I saw a pizza restaurant a few blocks from here. I could get pizza and salad."

"Good. I'll shower and be in a better mood when you get back."

*   *   *

Just as Alexis stepped out of the shower, the phone rang.

"Aunt Georgia. Thank goodness you called."

"Alexi, where are you?"

"In Athens, at Vaso's. Theo and I have had quite an adventure in the past couple of days. It's too long a story to tell you on the phone."

"Is it about Panayiotis?"

"Yes. Panayiotis is in jail."

"Oh, *bravo*, Alexi. I'm so relieved. I want to hear everything."

"First, I need to ask you something."

"Yes, dear."

"Do you know who lives in Diana's apartment building?"

"The ground floor is offices. Diana's neighbor on the second floor is Simeon Laurentis. You met him at Diana's party last year. Remember the charming conversation about immigrants?"

"God, yes. He was the man shouting about the crime rate. What does he do?"

"He *was* Minister of Culture two governments ago when the conservatives were in power. After that, he went to Munich—or was it Zurich? Came back perhaps three years ago. Strange man, no family, a gorgeous villa on the island of Evia. Or so I hear. Why?"

Alexis felt her pulse rate jump. "Minister of Culture? Why him?"

"I suppose he contributed heavily to the party. He has tons of money, inherited wealth from shipyards."

"Why the Ministry of Culture?"

"Oh, he's an amateur archeologist. He did a lot to establish regional museums around Greece."

While helping himself to some of the finds, Alexis guessed. "How well do you know him, Aunt Georgia?"

"He's reclusive. Nobody *knows* him. I've been introduced at Diana's parties. He never invites anyone. The only person who really talks to him is Petros. Same obsession. Now, why are you so interested in Simeon Laurentis?"

Alexis hesitated. "He could be part of the story with Panayiotis." The doorbell rang. "There's Theo with lunch. Hold on just a minute."

She ran to the door, yanked Theo inside. "You won't believe this." She dashed back to the phone. "Aunt Georgia, one more thing. Can you get into Diana's building?"

"Of course. I have keys for emergencies."

"And you're not going anywhere in the next twenty-four hours?"

"I'll be right here. Alexi, you're not doing anything dangerous, are you?"

"Is Laurentis dangerous?"

"Hardly. Eccentric, not dangerous."

"Aunt Georgia, please don't mention this conversation to anyone."

"I'm not going to get any more out of you?"

"Not just yet, but soon."

"Promise?"

"I promise."

Theo waited, a large pizza box in his hands, for her news.

"It looks like I had the wrong apartment after all. Diana's neighbor, Simeon Laurentis, is an ex-Minister of Culture who happens to be an avid archeologist."

"From that you conclude—"

"Minister of Culture is a perfect—if high risk—cover for dealing in antiquities. Laurentis knows the field, the authorities; he has contacts overseas." She piled her hair on her head, shook it out. "I'd give a lot to get into that apartment. He must have quite a collection."

"You got all that from Georgia?"

"I made a few inferences." She guided him toward the kitchen table. "The smell from that box is driving me crazy. Let's eat, then talk."

Alexis put out plates, dug into the pizza. "Let's say Laurentis *is* our dealer. It wouldn't be enough for us to expose his collection."

"Why not?"

"Stolen objects can be disguised or legitimized. Surely, he's taken precautions. What we need to do is catch him in the act of receiving stolen goods."

"Impossible—and dangerous."

She ignored his warning. "Suppose I call him, say I'm a friend of Nitsa's and want to deliver the head."

"Why wouldn't Nitsa deliver it?"

"She's being watched by the police."

"Okay. Then what?"

"He takes the head and we report Laurentis to the police. He's exposed and his smuggling career's over."

"*Ela.* If this man's as well connected as you say, he'll call off the police. A former minister's word against yours—a foreigner and a police suspect?"

Frustrated, Alexis tore into another slice of pizza. "What do you suggest?"

"We need evidence. Like catching a spy. We'd have to photograph him in the act."

"That would be entrapment."

"Alexi, I don't—"

"He's going to pay for the head, isn't he?" She rushed on. "I'll ask him for half the money now and a signed note for the other half to be delivered when I—"

Theo broke into a grin. "When you bring him the other head."

"What other head?"

"Didn't you tell Panayiotis there were two?"

"*Yes.*" She wiped her mouth, blew him a kiss. "I may have to improvise, but I'm going to call him." She searched the phone book on Vaso's desk. "Here it is. Rigillis."

Behind her, Theo warned, "Don't use his name, Alexi. I'm sure Nitsa didn't know it. Don't use yours either."

Alexis nodded and dialed. "Good afternoon. I want to speak to the owner of the house."

"Who's calling?" a female voice said.

"A business associate. Is he there?"

"Mr. Laurentis is away. I will be speaking to him later. What message can I give him?"

"I need to speak with him about a delivery. It's urgent. Do you have his number?"

"I can't give out his phone number. He'll call you."

"I'm calling from a kiosk. Look, your boss gave me this number. He asked me to be in contact."

The maid hesitated, then gave her a number in Evia to call after six p.m.

Alexis hung up, trembling. An attack of nerves. She paced in front of the sofa where Theo had stretched out. "Could we rehearse this phone call?"

"I'm Laurentis?"

"Yes." She cleared her throat. "Sir, I have something from Serros for you."

Theo grumbled, "Who is this?"

"A friend of Nitsa's. She can't contact you."

"Why not?"

"She's being watched. Panayiotis is in jail."

"Stupid fools."

"Nitsa has two marble heads from Serros. She wants the money for one now. You'll get the other when you get Panayiotis out of jail."

Theo nodded. "That's just what Nitsa would say."

"Good." Alexis hesitated. "What if Nitsa warned Laurentis?"

"I doubt it. After all, the maid said nothing and gave you his number."

"Okay, back to the phone call. Lisa, Nitsa's friend, speaking— I want the money today and a note saying you'll pay for the other delivery within two weeks."

"A note? Ridiculous. What for?"

"Nitsa wants insurance you'll get Panayiotis out. No note, no head."

"I guess it's worth a try." Theo looked skeptical. He stood up, rubbed her neck and shoulder.

"That feels fantastic."

He smiled. "Let's take a rest. When you call Laurentis, you need to be relaxed."

"If he's there."

"He'll be there. I'm sure the maid's already contacted him."

CHAPTER 18

Alexis sprang off Vaso's bed when the alarm beeped.

Theo sleepily checked his watch, gave her a thumbs-up. "Six o'clock."

"I'll wait ten minutes," she said. "I don't want to appear too eager."

She threw on a yellow and white striped blouse and navy slacks, rehearsed the phone call in her mind, then dialed Evia. "Hello. This is Nitsa's friend calling."

"You are not Greek." The voice was cold, clipped.

"Swedish. I'm to make a delivery."

"Stupid girl. Not over the phone. Where is Nitsa?"

"At home. She couldn't come—for obvious reasons."

"Such as?"

"The police are watching her. Panayiotis is in jail."

"What?" he barked.

"Nitsa said to tell you there were problems. Arrests. She only has a small part—but the best part—of the shipment. I need to deliver it today, before she's searched."

"This doesn't sound right."

Alexis rushed on. "She's got to get Panayiotis out. She's giving you one part now, the rest, when he's free."

"Nitsa thinks she's running the show, does she?"

"No. She's desperate. It takes money."

"Panayiotis can rot in jail."

"Nitsa thinks he might talk."

A long pause. Had she blown it? "You don't want the package?"

"I didn't say that."

"If I bring you the package, I need half the money now and a signed note saying you'll pay the rest with the next delivery."

"Absurd. Go by the apartment now. Leave the package. There'll be ten million drachma waiting with my maid. Tell Nitsa to await my instructions."

Alexis stared at the receiver in her hand. "He hung up. He's paying the money, but he refused to sign a note."

"I didn't think he would," Theo said.

"Damn. I'm doing it again—turning over the head for nothing in return."

"Not nothing. We'll get a look at his place. Anyway, why not turn over something else?"

"Like what?"

"Like anything. A jar of olives. The maid won't unwrap the package."

*   *   *

Once again disguised in a scarf and oversized sunglasses, Alexis rang the downstairs bell of the elegant neoclassical. "Delivery."

She was buzzed in.

"I'm incredibly nervous," Alexis whispered to Theo above the clanging of the venerable wood-paneled elevator.

An oval glass table with black lacquered chairs on either side adorned the second floor landing. To the right was Diana's apartment; to the left, Laurentis'. In front of his carved wood door was an elegant wrought-iron gate. Alexis hadn't noticed it when she'd been there before as it fit the style of the landing. Now she understood its purpose.

The white-haired maid, a burgundy birthmark on one side of her face, pulled open the door and scrutinized them through the gate. "Put the package on the table, please. I'll pass you the money. If you don't leave the package, I'll set off the alarm and you'll be stopped."

"You don't seem to trust us." Alexis placed her package on the table. "I want to count the money."

"As you wish." The maid passed a thick manila envelope through the gate.

Alexis sat down on one of the chairs, glanced down at the marble floor. Executing their plan was not going to be pleasant. "Ten thousand, twenty, thirty . . . " She grabbed the edge of the table and cried, "Oh, my God." She dropped in a heap on the floor.

"Lisa, Lisa." Theo held her to him, shouted to the maid. "Open the door. Quickly."

The maid gasped, swung open the iron gate.

Theo rushed in, Alexis moaning in his arms. "The sofa?"

The maid pointed, speechless, to the living room where Theo laid Alexis down, removed her sandals.

"We must revive her. Please bring water."

The maid rushed out.

"Alexi, look at this room."

Floor-to-ceiling cases covered the walls, displaying shelf after shelf of artifacts. They were hard to make out in the evening light, but it was clearly a collection fit for a museum.

Theo hissed, "She's coming back."

The maid brought over a water glass. Theo supported Alexis with one arm, helped her drink. She tried to swallow, choked, spouting water all over. It was no act. "I'm sorry. I'm so dizzy."

The maid put a towel to her forehead.

"Thank you," Alexis said. "I get heart palpitations, especially in the heat. I'll be okay in a few minutes." She drank some more, grabbed the maid's arm. "Could I have more water? And some light to count the money?"

The maid bustled off. The lights in the cases came on.

Alexis surveyed the room again. "Christ, Theo, he can't have legitimized *all* of this. We've got to come back with a camera."

"Right now we've got to get out of here."

The maid returned with a second glass of water.

After Alexis drank it down, she said, "I know you wouldn't cheat us. We'll just take the money and leave."

The maid crossed herself in gratitude. "My employer is very correct." She ushered them to the front door, took the package from the hall table and pulled the iron gate shut. She stood guard silently until they stepped into the elevator.

*   *   *

With most local restaurants closed for the holiday, Alexis suggested they eat at the Hilton Coffee Shop.

Theo studied the menu. "Everything is so expensive."

She caressed his hand. "Forget about the prices. We just sold a jar of olives for thirty thousand dollars."

He looked so worried she broke up in laughter. "We'll return the money. We can still eat whatever we want. I have a credit card with me."

They ordered t-bone steaks and salad. Theo swore he'd never tasted meat like that before.

Alexis was too hyper to eat. "So, what do you think now about Simeon Lauentis?"

"Disgusting."

Alexis was glad to see him fired up. "How do we get back into the apartment?"

"We have to divert the maid."

"Agreed. I was thinking about Georgia."

Theo nodded. "So was I. But even if we somehow neutralize the maid and take photographs, then what? Laurentis can obstruct a police investigation."

"The newspapers. If the press gets hold of this story, especially the pro-government press, it won't drop it until the ex-Minister of Culture goes to jail." Alexis spoke with more assurance than she felt.

"We'd look pretty foolish calling in the press, then finding out Laurentis is legitimate."

"We need a professional opinion. Petros won't want to help, but he'll look pretty foolish if he doesn't. Smuggling? Right under the up-and-coming archeologist's nose?"

"We still have to get in."

Alexis pushed her plate away. "I'm sure Georgia won't mind coming to town for a little excitement."

* * *

Georgia had hopped in her car as soon as she got their call. On the way to Diana's, Alexis filled her in on capturing the yacht and faking their way into Laurentis' apartment.

"An incredible story," she whooped. "I always thought Simeon was strangely secretive."

Georgia turned a brass key in the shiny lock on the front door, ushered them to the ancient elevator. At the second floor landing, she made sure there was no sign of Laurentis' maid, then disarmed the apartment alarm with another key and motioned Alexis and Theo inside.

The living room was filled with an opulent assortment of antiques and modern pieces. Georgia threw open the French doors. "We'd better not show ourselves on the veranda, even though it's beastly hot."

Theo sorted through the cameras Georgia had brought with her. "What's this?"

"A Polaroid. It makes instant pictures. Let me show you." She snapped his picture. "Now we wait three minutes."

Theo stared at the black box. When the photo began to appear, he looked disappointed. "It didn't work."

"It's not ready. It needs a minute to finish developing."

"Come on, you two," Alexis pleaded. "We have work to do."

The three sat down at the ebony card table in the corner of the room, Theo, intently watching the photo.

"See," Georgia said, "it turned out perfectly. Handsome devil."

Theo held the print before him. "Amazing."

"Very useful for tomorrow," Alexis said, drumming her fingers on the table. "*If* we get into the apartment."

"We will." Georgia's face flushed pink. "In the morning, I'll ask the maid to do some work for me and wave a lot of money in her face. While she's cleaning up in here, you can take your photos."

Alexis frowned. "If she sees the two of us again, she won't budge."

"And if we go in through a door or window, the alarm might go off," Theo said.

"The alarm will certainly go off. Every door and window is wired in the entire building. If anyone gets into one apartment, alarms go off in every apartment."

Alexis sighed. "Then it's hopeless."

Georgia arched her eyebrow. "Not at all. You'll go in through the front door."

"Impossible. Even if you get the maid to leave it open, we can't just walk by her and waltz into the apartment."

"How much time do you and Theo need to photograph? Ten minutes? I'll lock her in the kitchen and make a big show of trying to find the keys. You finish, I let her out."

"The kitchen door locks?"

Georgia jingled the key chain. "My dear, in these old houses, they had locks on everything."

"Wait. You two are moving too fast," Theo said. "The maid could refuse to leave the apartment unlocked."

Georgia smirked. "That's no problem. I get her to put her things down, *then* lock her in the kitchen."

"Aunt Georgia, you're a natural-born schemer," Alexis chirped. "Still, I detect a flaw in this plan. What if the maid puts the keys in her pocket?"

"I'm prepared to wrestle her." Georgia rose. "I'm going to watch the late news in the study."

Alexis grinned at Theo. "She's something. We'll have assault to add to our crimes."

"Alexi, we're not committing any crimes. I suggest we put the money back when we go in." He crossed his arms. "Laurentis has broken the law. We're just taking photographs."

"You've gotten more committed to this venture."

"No man should have a private collection like that."

"Not if he obtained it illegally."

"Even legally."

Alexis wondered if his remark came from growing up under communism. "There's still a chance he's legitimized all his stuff."

"Then why would he be dealing with Panayiotis?"

"True. Just in case, I suggest we photograph the head of Artemis to show Laurentis acquired at least one newly stolen object."

"As long as we don't leave it there."

From the study, Georgia screeched, "Come quick. They're talking about Serros."

The announcer reported a successful attempt by local fishermen to stop an antiquities smuggling ring using one of the island's harbors. Several *kaikis* chased the smugglers straight into the arms of the Coast Guard. The organizer of the operation, an Albanian immigrant, was going to collect a reward from the government.

Georgia clapped her hands. "Theo, did you hear that?"

"They didn't get it right. It was a blockade, not a chase."

"The reward. You're going to get a reward," Georgia crowed.

"The fishermen deserve the reward. They were the ones who took the risks, not me."

"Theo, that's too noble. It was your idea and you took plenty of risks."

Alexis waved her hands. "You two are missing something. This newscast could be bad for us. What if Laurentis hears it?"

"He already knows there's been trouble from your phone call," Theo said. "This just confirms it."

"He could get nervous with the publicity." Alexis tensed. "We've got to photograph early tomorrow."

"How early?" Georgia asked.

"Eight at the latest."

"Eight! You have no idea what you're asking." She laughed excitedly as she clicked off the television. "Well, if you can get me up, I can do it."

CHAPTER 19

Georgia raced back into Diana's apartment, dropped onto the apricot velvet sofa. "Whew. What a negotiation." She wiped a trickle of perspiration from her temple.

Alexis and Theo emerged from their hiding place in the guest room.

"Report," Alexis said.

"Anna—that's the maid's name—is under strict orders not to leave the house. Can you imagine? She gets only one day off every two weeks? It's slavery. And she's been with Laurentis for years. Anyway, she seemed genuinely sorry she couldn't help me. I told her I was desperate and took out my wallet, which she eyed hungrily."

"Aunt Georgia, you're making this into a soap opera."

"Sorry. Anna needs money for her grandson's baptism. She's coming over in an hour, after her morning call from Laurentis, to light the oven and clean. She and I are sworn to secrecy."

Alexis exhaled loudly. "You did it."

"It's not done yet. I'll go back over, just before nine, ask her to bring some cleaning materials and suggest she leave the apartment door open so she can hear the phone."

"Did you explain why you're here?"

"Oh, she knows I'm Diana's sister-in-law."

For the next hour, Alexis watched for the maid through the peephole in the front door, while Theo stood guard at the window, checking the street.

"Georgia," he said, "let's go over this one more time."

"Everyone has the same alarm system," she said. "You disarm Laurentis' alarm the same as here—at the box outside the apartment door."

"And the back door?" Theo asked.

"It opens onto the stairs down to the garage. There's an alley to the street. The elevator also goes to the garage."

Georgia looked at her watch. "Ten to nine. Places."

Alexis and Theo retreated to their hiding place. This time Georgia was gone longer. They listened through a crack in the door.

"Anna, I must have some coffee."

It sounded like a broom dropped to the floor. "Oh dear. Why didn't you tell me? I would have brought you some."

"Thank you. I like my own coffee. If only we can get the oven to work. I'm so hopeless with these things."

Steps moving toward the kitchen.

"It must be the pilot light," Anna said.

"Indeed," Alexis whispered to Theo, who'd extinguished the pilot light after their early breakfast.

They heard the kitchen door close, the key grinding in the lock.

Moments later, Georgia thrust open the guest room door and mouthed, "Now."

Loaded with cameras, Laurentis' money, and the marble head in a backpack, Alexis and Theo hurried across the landing. Anna had left her keys hanging from the lock of the wrought-iron gate. "Couldn't be better," Alexis murmured.

They disarmed the alarm system, waited a full minute, then made directly for the living room. A light switch by the door turned on the lamps, but not the lighting in the cases.

"We have to find those lights," Alexis muttered, "or the photos won't come out. I don't see switches anywhere."

They searched the living room and large columned hall. "Why didn't we think of this?" Her voice quavered.

"Alexi, when you collapsed, Anna turned the lights on when she went for water. They must be near the kitchen."

They crossed the dining room to the swinging doorway to the

kitchen. No switches. Theo studied the paneling. Pressing on a newer looking piece of wood, he released a small cupboard door with a row of switches inside.

"These could trigger another alarm," Alexis said.

"No choice. Go see what happens."

Lights flickered on in several cases in the living room.

Alexis let out her breath. "That's it," she called. "Throw all the switches."

She grabbed her backpack from the desk, removed the head from the burlap bag. "We've lost five minutes. Let's do Artemis first—with the Polaroid."

She placed the goddess, her playful smile looking out, on an ornate coffee table next to a photograph of Laurentis receiving an award. "No doubt whose living room this is."

They moved methodically around the room. The upper shelves were too high to photograph, but they had enough without them.

Alexis returned to the main case. "I might as well finish this roll."

Suddenly, Theo seized her arm, clapped his hand over her mouth. Alexis froze. She'd heard what he'd heard—the clanking of the elevator. The motor hummed.

Theo pointed to the kitchen, grabbed the cameras and backpack. They darted through the kitchen's swinging door.

"Laurentis," Alexis whispered. "You've got to disappear. Take the cameras and head before he figures out what's happened."

"Come with me."

"No, I'll stall him. I can't leave Georgia alone." Alexis undid the two heavy locks on the kitchen door. "Theo, please, before the police come. Go to Vaso's first. Put the Polaroids in her mailbox. Then get to Peristeri as fast as you can."

The elevator door creaked open on the landing, followed by several thuds as if Laurentis were unloading.

Theo squeezed her shoulder. "Alexi, the man will be enraged. Go to Georgia."

"I will. Run."

He bolted down the back stairs. Alexis re-locked the door behind him, stood next the swinging door, straining to hear. She caught a muffled male voice swearing.

She'd play Lisa. Maybe he'd believe she'd come to talk to him, to get help for Nitsa.

Where was he anyway? Alexis pushed the door open slightly. Shouts echoed from Diana's apartment. My God, he was yelling at Georgia.

She slipped into the hall, hid behind the one of the columns. Brisk footsteps. A man strode into the apartment, followed by a wailing Anna. He headed right for the living room.

As Alexis stepped from behind the column, Anna screamed. Laurentis whirled around, grasped Alexis' arm. "What the hell is going on?"

"I came to see you about the other head. Nitsa needs the money."

"You lie easily, but I'm only fooled once." He twisted her arm behind her back with ferocious force and propelled her toward Diana's apartment.

Ear to the phone, Georgia said emphatically, "Now." When she caught sight of Laurentis, she shouted, "Let go of my niece. Simeon, that was Petros. He's just back from the country. He'll be right over to straighten this out."

Laurentis—piercing black eyes, aquiline nose, silver hair— looked like a bird of prey ready to swoop down on its next victim. Georgia removed herself to the couch. Laurentis shoved Alexis toward her.

"Next, the police." Smirking, he crossed to the phone on the antique desk. "Let's see—breaking and entering, attempted robbery. I mustn't forget Anna. Kidnapping as well."

Alexis told herself he was bluffing. They'd done nothing more than enter his apartment and take some photographs. Nothing compared to his crimes.

Georgia obviously saw it the same way. "Simeon, you'll be deeply sorry if you call the police. You'll serve a long sentence for the things in that collection."

He look startled for no more than a second or two. "You don't really think I'll have problems with the police. The ones I'm calling already work for me."

"You'll have problems when they see your latest acquisition. It's all over the news," Georgia spat out.

Alexis flashed her a look, but too late.

Cold rage froze Laurentis' sharp features in place. "Anna," he shouted. "Bring the package."

The maid, eyes swollen, her birthmark livid, scurried in.

"Open it."

She struggled with the tape, grabbed the letter opener from the desk. As she pulled the olive jar from the wad of newspaper, she let out a wail.

Laurentis' nostrils quivered. "The head, I presume. Anna, remove that jar, but don't discard it."

"You didn't think we'd sell you the real thing, did you?" Alexis said scornfully. "The money's in your living room."

"I wouldn't put it past you to try to sell it twice."

The elevator clanged again. Georgia patted Alexis' hand to reassure her.

"Ah, Mr. Diamandopoulos, just in time." Laurentis crossed his arms over his chest. "Look what we have here. Your aunt and her niece have broken into my apartment, kidnapped my maid, and engaged in a fraudulent sale of allegedly stolen antiquities. No doubt they would have looted my collection if I hadn't walked in on them."

Alexis fired back. "That's bullshit and you know it."

"Alexis, you must be crazy," Petros said.

Laurentis laughed scornfully. "I thought this might be the young woman I once met at your mother's. Your girlfriend."

"That's long in the past." Petros planted himself in front of Alexis. "Where's the Albanian?"

"Ah, the missing link." Laurentis pulled out a chair, crossed his long legs. "Anna mentioned a male cohort. An Albanian? Even better. He's obviously fled the scene. The question is where and with what? The famous head, perhaps?"

Petros shook Alexis' shoulder. "Where is he?"

"Petros, you can't cooperate with this man. He's a thief."

Petros faced Laurentis. "The Albanian might be in Pangrati. Alexis stays there at a friend's. I can give you the address."

Alexis shivered at his betrayal, so open, so callous.

Laurentis rose. "Ladies, you will be detained here until the police find your co-conspirator. They will arrest him, but I shall suggest leniency—expelling him from Greece. After they're through, he won't want to return. Mr. Diamandopoulos, kindly cut the phone line, collect their cellulars and keys."

The two women watched speechlessly as Petros followed orders.

"Be sure to set the outside alarm, so I know if they try to escape." Laurentis looked back at Alexis and Georgia. "I'm stationing a policeman downstairs should you consider jumping."

"This is for your own good," Petros muttered as he stalked out.

Alexis felt as if she'd been punched in the stomach. The police would now search for Theo. They might pick him up in Pangrati. She was to blame. She'd told him to put the photos in Vaso's mailbox. He had the head. If they caught him, he'd be charged with stealing antiquities.

"Is it as bad as I think?" she said to Georgia, her voice leaden.

"Alexi, darling, they may not find Theo," Georgia said taking her hand. "Even if they do—Well, Laurentis can't keep us here for long. As soon as we're free, we'll go to Maria and Nikos."

"By then, Theo will be a near-corpse tossed across the border."

Georgia's eyes filled. "I'm so sorry." She rummaged through her purse for a handkerchief.

"Aunt Georgia, can you believe that Petros . . . "

She sighed heavily. "It seems he knew about the collection."

"I can't believe it. Despite all his other weaknesses, he was devoted to archeology. He seemed so principled."

"People aren't weak in their personal lives and strong in their professional lives. It's all a question of character. Petros' character never fully formed. He never had a chance."

"Can we talk sense into him?"

"I just don't know. He's been hurting since you moved to Serros. Now he's got an outlet for his pain—Theo."

Alexis shuddered.

"Alexi, Theo has a good chance of getting away. He's very clever, you know. Let's make some coffee to clear our heads."

A half hour later, Alexis and Georgia had gotten nowhere. They had no way out of the apartment, no way to communicate with the outside world.

The two women sat forlornly listening to the ticking of the ormolu clock on the green marble fireplace. Alexis wallowed in self-recrimination. She'd been so cocky, so sure she could beat an art thief at his own game. If she'd left things alone, Theo would be a hero right now instead of on the run.

Voices on the landing, a key in the lock. Petros came marching in, a cruel smile on his face. "Your Albanian was picked up in Pangrati boarding a bus to Peristeri. He had the statue on him."

Alexis felt like clawing his face. She struggled for control. "For God's sake, don't you see how bad this is for *you*? You, the future star of Greek archeology, have lived for years next door to a dealer, yet you know nothing about his illegal collection? *I* find that hard to swallow. I can just imagine what your colleagues will think, to say nothing of the press."

"No one will ever find out until Laurentis dies. Then, it won't matter."

Desperate, Alexis tried another tack. "Think about the Serros marbles. They confirm your theory. The head is Artemis."

"Since when did you become such an expert?"

"I'm not. *You* figured out the misidentification of the temple. You can tell the world, but not if you're conspiring with Laurentis."

"There's no way to link Laurentis to Serros except your idiotic attempt to sell him the head. No one will believe you."

Georgia broke in. "My dear nephew, you're wrong. Panayiotis

is in jail. To save his own neck, he'll identify Laurentis. You'll be left holding the bag."

"You're both naive. Don't you think Laurentis has that covered?" Petros looked disgusted, stomped out.

Georgia put her arm around Alexis. "We gave him something to think about. He'll be back."

"Before or after the police teach Theo a lesson?" Alexis buried her head on Georgia's shoulder. "Why couldn't I leave well enough alone? Why did I have to go after Laurentis?"

"Because you're committed to the truth, Alexi. That's who you are. That's what makes you such a good friend and teacher and person. Now don't give up. We're going to get out of this."

An hour or so passed until they again heard sounds in the hall. Alexis sprang to the peephole. Laurentis was moving cartons from his apartment to the landing.

"Aunt Georgia, come quick."

"What's he doing?"

"He's taking away his stolen pieces." Alexis was suddenly raging mad. "Theo becomes the scapegoat and the villain gets away."

She began to pace. Laurentis had completely outsmarted them. Never before—not in her confrontations with Loukas, not in jail, not while in Panayiotis' clutches—had she felt so helpless. It was worse than waiting for the fire.

The fire. Her thoughts shot back to Serros, to the fire winding its way around the island to the east, then whooshing through the valley.

She marched over to the entrance hall, studied the polished oak front door, guest closet, French doors opening into the living room. On her knees, her cheek on the marble tiles, she examined the crack at the bottom of the front door. She could see the light on the landing. It just might work. What else did they have?

"Aunt Georgia, I have an idea. Succeed or fail, it would definitely get you in trouble with Diana."

"Why should I worry about Diana? She's my sister-in-law, but she's been aiding and abetting a criminal."

Alexis laughed softly. "Then, you're with me?"

"Of course. What are we going to do?"

"We're going to fight fire with fire."

CHAPTER 20

"Urban arsonist," Georgia exclaimed. "That's one role I never expected to play."

Alexis sent her a quick grin. "In the bosom of the establishment! Hurry. We need the most flammable material we can find."

"In the study. Diana has a stack of fake logs by the fireplace and that stuff you pour on to make flames."

"Lighter fluid. Terrific. We need lots of paper to get the fire started."

Georgia was loading up with logs. "Diana's collection of *Architectural Digests*." She crowed, "She'll be furious."

"I'm going to the pantry for paper goods."

In the front hall, the two women amassed a considerable pile in just a few minutes. The small vestibule seemed perfect for a bonfire.

Georgia removed the framed prints from the wall and the fur coats from the guest closet. "Diana should thank me except she'd probably rather have a new wardrobe."

"Aunt Georgia, we're going to need some wood in reserve. Those nested tables over there would be good and the plant stands. I know they're antiques—"

"Alexi, we're prisoners. Theo's in the hands of the police. Laurentis is escaping. It's now or never."

"I'm going for the floor fan in the guest room."

When Alexis came back, she broke the panes of glass at the bottom of the French doors with a hammer. Once the fire got going, the fan would blow flames and smoke under the front door and onto the landing, perhaps to Laurentis' apartment. At least, in theory. Even a small conflagration should set off the alarms, bring the fire department.

"Careful with that broken glass, Alexi. I'm going to put the chain on the door in case anyone tries to stop us."

"Then we can't get out."

"My dear, we're not going out that way."

They built a pyramid of crumpled magazine pages and balled up paper towels, encircled, like a maypole, by streamers of toilet paper. The logs stood at the ready. The two women stepped back to admire their work.

"Brilliant idea about the fan," Georgia said. "Where'd you learn about wind tunnels?"

"Serros. Where else?"

"Alexi, once the Fire Department gets here, you need to phone Maria and Nikos immediately. Take the keys to my place. It's closer than Vaso's. I'll handle things here."

"Okay." Alexis peered through the peephole. "Laurentis must still be downstairs loading his car. Remember, if this goes wrong and the fire comes this way, we run to the veranda, throw over the mattresses and jump."

The first look of hesitation crossed Georgia's face. "A trapeze artist I'm not."

They lit matches at various points around the edge of the pile. It began to smoke.

"Stand back," Alexis said. "I'm going to add the lighter fluid."

The fire caught with a whoosh and burst into flame. She gave it seconds, then tossed on the logs. They ignited quickly, flames shooting up. Georgia started the fan blowing through the broken glass.

Although they could see the torch-like flames, there was nothing except the sound of the fan.

"The door's thicker than I thought," Alexis moaned. "Why doesn't the damn smoke detector set off the alarm?"

"Patience, Alexi. If the smoke isn't coming in here, it's going somewhere. We may have to start piling on the furniture."

As if on cue, a shrill whistle broke the quiet of the morning, followed by three ear-splitting claxon sounds, then the whistle again.

Georgia raised her arms in triumph. "That's it. That awful noise will keep going until the fire's out. To the veranda."

They flung open the veranda doors. Alexis pulled the mattresses toward the stone balustrade.

"I'm not jumping unless the fire is licking at my heels," Georgia declared.

"I'm just as scared as you are." Leaning over the balustrade, Alexis shouted, "Look. Quick. A silver Mercedes leaving the garage. Laurentis escaping."

"We should have figured on that. Is that Petros running down the street? Yes. Will he save us or leave us to burn like witches?"

"Not funny, Aunt Georgia. God. Anna. I bet Laurentis left her in the apartment."

The two women started yelling at the policeman below who was already pushing back curious neighbors. Petros dashed up, said something to the policeman, then shouted. "The fire department's coming. For God's sake, don't jump. They'll have a ladder."

"The fire's in the front hall," Alexis shouted over the din. "You've got to go up the back stairs and get the maid."

Petros disappeared.

"Thank God, he's got some humanity left." Georgia looked down, waved to the crowd below which shouted encouragement. "Alexi, we're stars."

"Aunt Georgia, you're enjoying this."

"I'm also watching for the fire truck. Ah, finally."

Alexis realized she needed to remove some of the evidence. Now that the firemen had arrived, she could risk turning off the fan. She unplugged it, dragged it, hands burning, into the guest room. She then moved the reserve furniture back into place.

A steel ladder appeared against the balustrade. A fireman

hoisted Georgia onto the wide stone ledge, instructed her where to put her feet.

"Alexi, I can't resist this moment of glory. See you downstairs." Georgia climbed down to the cheers of the crowd. At the bottom, she gave a victory sign and beckoned to Alexis, who, trembling, followed her stalwart example.

Georgia turned to the fireman in charge, gave him a kiss on the cheek to more cheers. "That was brilliant. Now, I'm sending my niece to my apartment near here to call the insurance company. I'll stay here as long as necessary."

He nodded.

"Go," Georgia commanded Alexis, just as Petros came out of the alley with a bawling Anna.

* * *

Maria picked up on the first ring. "Alexi, where are you?"

"At Georgia's in Kolonaki. There's been a fire at Diana's. The police picked up Theo. Laurentis is trying to throw him out of the country."

"Calm down, Alexi. We're on it. Theo called us from jail, just as we were leaving for the country. Nikos is down there." She chortled. "The police are wondering how to arrest a national hero who has just tracked down a major art thief."

"But the police take orders from Laurentis."

"Only some, and only behind closed doors. Nikos called our friend, Vangelis Stamakos, from the *Free Press*, to join him. It's a fantastic scoop. Now what's this about a fire?"

Alexis threw herself back on the couch, closed her eyes. "Theo's all right? He'll be freed?"

"Of course. Listen, you can tell me about the fire later. Can you get the photos from Vaso's? Now?"

"Yes. And then?"

"We'll meet up at the office. Then, we'll call on Mr. Laurentis."

"He left in his car loaded with antiquities."

"We'll track him down. Alexi, the photos are critical."

"I'm on my way."

*   *   *

Maria plucked a photo out of the pile. "This is the one for the newspapers—the head next to the photo of Laurentis. It's fabulous."

Alexis rubbed ointment on her blistered hands. "How soon will Theo be here?"

"Ten minutes at most." Maria stared at the photo. "Do you realize what a story this is?"

"I honestly don't care. I just hope they catch Laurentis."

"Alexi, you'd better expect some major publicity. This is the harvest of the decade."

"The last thing I want is publicity."

"You may not want it, but it will happen."

"I'll hide away in Serros."

Maria chortled. "That's the last place you could hide. You know, you've become a very bad client. You didn't follow my advice about the head, but for once I'm glad."

Alexis heard the front door opening, flew into the reception area. Theo looked disheveled but all in one piece. He swept her in his arms.

"Did they beat you?" she murmured.

"They roughed me up a little, but once Nikos spoke to them, they backed off. How'd they know where to find me?"

"Petros showed up. He actually helped Laurentis."

Maria strode into the hall. "No fair. We all want the whole story. The coffee's made. Come inside."

Alexis kissed Theo one more time, led him into the office. She threw her arms around Nikos. "Thank you. Twice to the rescue."

He looked flustered by her display of affection. "A pleasure. This is our friend, Vangelis Stamakos."

Alexis shook hands with the young, pudgy journalist. "I can't give you the whole story."

"I'm only interested in Laurentis."

Alexis smiled. "That part you can have. Gladly. Just don't ever report how we baited him with a marble head."

"You want it for your memoirs," Stamakos said, an impish look on his face.

"Absolutely not. I want to put the whole thing behind me." She looked at Theo, not wanting to speak for him.

He nodded. "Agreed."

Alexis recounted their pursuit of Laurentis. Maria let out a howl of delight when Alexis got to the part about the olive jar. "Now that's smart."

"Theo's idea."

When Alexis got to the end, Nikos leaned forward, a look of amazement on his face. "You and Georgia set a fire?"

"Nothing to it."

Grinning, Theo turned to Alexis. "I need to get back. Laurentis is *your* man. As soon as you get free, come to Nemea."

"Yes. It's better that you leave. The police could still try to get you for something."

Maria stood up. "Then Nikos will take the kids and drive Theo to Nemea. And Vangelis will finish up with Laurentis."

"And I must get back to Georgia," Alexis said, jumping up. "I can't leave her alone to face Diana's wrath."

CHAPTER 21

Diana's entrance hall looked remarkably intact. The oak door had been sanded, the walls were coated with primer. Some varnish and paint, and it would be like new.

"In the study, Alexis." Diana spoke coldly and in English, confirming Georgia's hurried telephone message that Diana was on the warpath.

Georgia sat drinking coffee at the antique table by the window. "*Kalimera*, Alexi *mou*." A conspiratorial smile flickered across her face.

Diana waved Alexis to a chair, made no offer of coffee. Imperiously, she tossed back her cascade of blonde-streaked hair. "I have finally figured out what went on this weekend. Between Petros, Anna, and the police, I believe I have the whole picture."

She glared first at Georgia, then Alexis. "You two used this apartment as a base of operations to snoop on my distinguished neighbor. You accused him of antiquities theft. When he caught you in the act, you set fire to the place."

Georgia put down her cup with a loud clink. "I'm glad you didn't say *falsely* accuse, Diana. As for the charge of arson, it would be more appropriate to accuse your son of imprisonment."

"Leave Petros out of this," she snapped.

Alexis was prepared with her own agenda. "Evidently, you were aware your distinguished neighbor had an antiquities collection."

"Naturally. Do you think I'm stupid?"

"On the contrary. I'm sure you know a great deal about Greek law," Alexis retorted. "Most of Laurentis' collection was obtained illegally."

"I did not check it for legality, Alexis. Simeon intended to give his collection to the Greek state at his death. He left a fortune to create a museum in his name. I find that extremely admirable. In point of fact, I designed the building's interior."

Of course, Alexis thought, she's in up to her ears. "Those antiquities belong to the Greek people. They should have been in the National Archeological Museum long ago."

"Where they'd languish in some dusty back room. You've seen the condition of the museum. Compared to an elegant private museum—well, there's no comparison."

"Do you understand what you've said, Diana?" Alexis was indignant. "That makes you a co-conspirator."

"You're hardly one to speak. First, you're accused of murder and actually go to jail. Then, you break into my apartment."

"Whoa," Georgia exclaimed. "Let's get the record straight. Alexis was *framed* for murder. I *invited* her to the apartment. Diana, you're verging on slander."

"You may call it whatever you like. I haven't finished. I charge you two with causing the death of a prominent and harmless man." She actually smiled victoriously.

There was an empty silence in the room.

Finally, Georgia said wearily, "Just tell us what happened."

"The Evia police found Simeon last night at his villa, a bullet through his head." She spat the words. "His suicide note left instructions regarding your precious antiquities."

Alexis covered her eyes with her hand. Georgia crossed over to her, gently pulled her up by the arm, then turned back to Diana. "I feel terrible about Simeon, but if anyone, besides himself, is to blame for his death, it's you and Petros. Instead of helping him deal with his obsessive sickness and criminal behavior, you protected him."

Alexis' long accumulated anger at Diana ignited. "You've ruined Petros, Diana. This will jeopardize his whole career."

Diana shouted, "I want you both out now. You can be sure this is not the end of it."

*   *   *

On the street, Georgia put her arm around Alexis, suggested they walk a bit.

"Aunt Georgia, did you know about Laurentis?"

"No, but it was the only way out for him. He could never have handled the shame. He certainly couldn't bear imprisonment."

"There must have been another way. I wish we'd thought it through."

"Alexi, he knew he'd be found out eventually. That's why he made such elaborate provisions for a museum—an attempt at cover."

"Still, we're responsible for what happened."

"That's what I love about you, Alexi. You don't run from anything."

Georgia's words unhinged Alexis. Tears streamed down her face. "Sorry, I . . . I'm crying about—"

"I know. Petros."

"He so lost. He needs help."

"I won't abandon him. I can't. He's my only nephew. But you mustn't grieve for him. Move on with your life."

Alexis dried her eyes with Georgia's proffered handkerchief. "Come home with me," Georgia said.

"I'd love to, but I've got an appointment at school at two."

"Lunch time? How uncivilized."

Alexis smiled weakly. "It's an uncivilized American school."

"Are you all right, *agapi mou?*"

"I don't know if I'm more angry or sad—like the day the kittens were poisoned. I'll get over it. Thank you for defending me with Diana."

"Don't be ridiculous. I can't stand her, but I must endure her. She's my sister-in-law by marriage." She hugged Alexis. "You're my niece by choice."

*   *   *

Alexis strode down the canary yellow hallway to the principal's office, its door newly painted with the colors of the rainbow. Gregory Hudson had doubtless come up with the bizarre paint scheme. In a stereotypically American way, the school principal was turning the place into a pot of gold.

Hudson stood in the reception area, hunched over a computer print-out. He looked up over his horn-rimmed half-glasses, marched like a bantam across the room, pushed open his office door. "Alexis, come in. You've had a difficult summer."

"I've had better, but at least things turned out all right."

"How is that?"

"I thought Lincoln's always the first to know. We've broken up an antiquities smuggling ring and caught the man who framed me for murder."

"I'd heard, yes. I also heard you caused a prominent Athenian to commit suicide."

Alexis looked at him with disgust. "That's the spin Diana Diamandopoulos puts on it."

He sat back, pushed his glasses onto his balding head. "I did speak with Mrs. Diamandopoulos. Whatever spin you put on it, it's bad for Lincoln."

"Look, Greg, I played a role in exposing Laurentis, but I didn't *cause* his suicide. He killed himself because he couldn't face being brought to justice."

"Alexis, I've spoken with the members of the Board. Let me be blunt. The consensus is you'd be more happily employed elsewhere."

Alexis gripped her chair. "You're firing me?"

"I suggest you resign. That way I can give you a letter of recommendation. Since it's too late to find another position for the fall, the Board has most generously agreed to pay you half your annual salary. Let's call it a gift of appreciation for your years of service."

"Do you think I'm going to walk away from here just because Diana Diamandopoulos is out to get me?"

"I didn't make myself clear. This is the Board's decision. They don't want you teaching here. They don't want any more negative publicity."

"You have no grounds. I have rights."

"Not many. This is a private school in a foreign country. You're actually quite vulnerable."

"You bastard."

"I'll disregard that. Let me urge you to consider your situation carefully. If you force me to fire you, if you go on some crusade, there'll be no compensation. If you choose to resign, I need a letter by the end of the week."

"I'm not going to make this easy. There are many teachers and parents who will support me."

"I don't think so, Alexis. The Albanian's the final straw for most of us."

Alexis sprang up and tore out the office, slamming the door. She charged down the hall to the bathroom, hung her head over the sink, threw cold water on her burning face. Staring at the mirror, she half-expected to see someone else.

This couldn't be happening. Teaching was her life. If she got fired from Lincoln, she'd lose her work permit; she'd never be hired anywhere else. If she resigned and left quietly, she'd be giving in to a vicious campaign. Hudson had her just where he wanted.

Always the first to rush to the defence of other teachers, Alexis wondered who would defend her. The Board was powerful. *They don't want you teaching here.* She felt like smashing the bathroom mirror.

She had to keep her feelings under control until she got back to Vaso's. She needed Vaso now, wished her loyal friend were back from her holiday. She headed to her classroom to grab her papers, suddenly stopped. If she removed anything now, they'd know she was quitting. She'd leave everything in place. Let them stew. She'd take her time figuring it all out.

*   *   *

Alexis collapsed on Vaso's bed. Anger flared every time she thought about the hypocritical Board members who'd conspired with Diana and Hudson. She should have seen it coming. Hudson had been gunning for her. Diana had played right into his hands, obviously trying to deflect attention from Petros. The board members also wanted the onus for Laurentis' death on Alexis. Laurentis was part of the establishment; better to blame the outsider.

The Albanian's the last straw. Alexis tasted the bile in the back of her throat. Bitter. Her life had turned bitter.

Was there a future for her in Greece? No school would hire her once the word got out. She could never live on private English lessons. She'd have to go back to the States, teach there. At least she could come back to the *liotrivi* in the summers. They couldn't take that from her.

And Theo? She knew she loved him, but he had to take care of his family, establish them in Greece. He'd been so ecstatic when he'd called yesterday. At Vassilis' urging, the Serros fishermen had decided he and Alexis should get all the reward money, admitting they'd only joined forces because of Theo.

Theo's half would be enough to get his family visas. Hers was to have replaced her nest egg. Now, she'd be using the money to support herself for a few more months. At least, she wouldn't have to leave right away. She'd have more time with Theo.

What an irony that just as he was settling down, she was being uprooted.

*   *   *

Alexis rolled over, gazed out Vaso's window. The street lamps had come on, casting pale halos on the ceiling. She'd fallen into a deep sleep.

Hungry, she fixed a ham and cheese sandwich in the kitchen,

washed it down with liberal amounts of *retsina*.

It was two weeks until the start of school. No need to tell anyone just yet she'd been fired. Hudson may have gotten rid of her, but why make it easy? Let him go nuts with worry. What was the Greek expression? Revenge is a dish best eaten cold.

There was another reason not to say anything right now. She didn't want to rain on Theo's parade. He'd planned a big party in Nemea on Saturday—a celebration.

Alexis emptied the jug into her wine glass. What did she have to show for her eight years in Greece? Friendships, a pretty good classical education, hordes of students who'd thrived in her classes. She had a beautiful home to which she could always return. The years hadn't been wasted.

She could rally her spirits temporarily, crawl back into her protective shell. But she couldn't deny the ache inside for what had become precious—putting down roots and committing to a man she loved.

She bit her lip. There was still unfinished business. She wasn't leaving without the last piece of the story. She would not let Laurentis take it with him to the grave.

CHAPTER 22

The next morning, Alexis sat impatiently in the waiting room of the jail. The dirty green walls, bars on the windows, sour smell of tobacco, all brought back jail time, only two months ago.

What was taking so long? Nitsa had insisted on talking to Panayiotis before Alexis confronted him. She said he'd cooperate sooner if *she* laid out the deal.

The door of the grimy anteroom flew open. "He'll see you," Nitsa said breathlessly, looking completely out of place in a bare-backed, orange sundress. "He's not in a very good mood, said we already made a deal."

"We did. No charges against you in exchange for Laurentis. But how did Panayiotis get the marbles?"

"I've told you a thousand times I don't know. Ask him." She looked around with distaste. "I don't want to wait here. Too depressing."

"Sit down, Nitsa. Enough is enough."

As had happened before, Nitsa, like a burst balloon, rapidly deflated. She dropped into a chair, her pink mouth dropping at the corners. She searched the room as if lost, then covered her face with her hands. "Panayiotis is a good boy. We had a nice life planned." Her voice broke, followed by a sob. "He was doing it for me."

Despite her irritation and disbelief, Alexis softened toward the woman. "If he treats you like he treated me, you're better off without him. But today isn't about revenge. If Panayiotis talks, he'll get out of jail a lot sooner."

"Why can't you leave it alone?"

"I've got to know the whole story."

*   *   *

A sullen Panayiotis sat slumped in a beat-up white plastic chair, his bandaged leg dangling over the arm. His rugged features were dulled by a heavy growth of beard. But if a week in prison had caused him regrets, he showed no sign of it.

Alexis welcomed the glass barrier between them. "Nitsa says you're ready to talk."

"What talk? I gave you Laurentis. That was the deal."

"In fact, Nitsa gave us Laurentis and that was only part of the deal. You tell me the whole story, I won't charge you with kidnapping."

Panayiotis eyed her. "How do I know you won't change your mind?"

"Here's your insurance—a sworn statement prepared by my lawyer clearing you of any kidnapping charges I might bring." She held the statement to the glass. "It's yours as soon as you talk."

He glanced at the statement, too stubborn to move closer to read it. Feigning boredom, he said, "Ask your questions."

"Laurentis. How did you know him?"

"I did some odd jobs for him in the past."

"When?"

"When he was Minister."

"What kind of odd jobs? Smuggling?"

He smirked. "Transportation."

"Inside or outside Greece?"

"Both."

"For how long?"

"I worked for him only a few years."

"But he'd been in the business . . ."

"A long time." Panayiotis snickered. "It picked up when he became minister."

Alexis felt renewed outrage at Laurentis' abuse of his office. "The marbles. How'd you get them?"

"I found them."

Alexis got up to leave. "You're doing yourself no good. Either you talk or I go—with the paper."

Panayiotis threw his head back, stared at the ceiling.

"Where'd you find the marbles? At the temple?" Alexis asked. "I've been up there many times. There were never any marbles lying around."

"They were hidden in the base behind one of the stones."

"How did you know that?"

"I had a diagram." He picked his tooth with a fingernail.

"Which Laurentis gave you."

"Yeah."

"Tell me about the diagram."

"What about it?"

"Was it old, new, in Greek?"

"Seems you already know. It was old. You could barely read it. It was in German." Panayiotis made a show of yawning. "Some German gave it to Laurentis. The German got it from his father, a Nazi, who was in Serros during the war."

"Where's the diagram now?"

"Are you crazy? I burned it. That's all I know. *All*. Now, give me the statement."

She held the paper over the document tray, ready to drop it, then took it back. "One last question. I've been living at the *liotrivi* since March. When did you have time to excavate?"

Panayiotis' smirk returned. "You forget you were in jail. Loukas, dead, was good for something," he said bitterly.

So framing her wasn't only to run her out of Serros; Panayiotis also desperately needed to get her away from the temple. Alexis flashed on the dream that had led her to the marbles. She'd been racing a man to the temple. This man before her.

With considerable regret, she dropped the paper in the tray.

*　　*　　*

Alexis nestled on the top deck of the ferry under a canvas of stars dotting the indigo sky. She pulled up the collar of her windbreaker. Autumn in the air. It went with the start of school—but not this year. She'd miss the kids, but she felt a certain relief she was out of Lincoln. She could almost say Hudson had done her a favor.

She thought about the meeting awaiting her. With Panayiotis' revelations, she was ninety-nine percent there. The German connection rang true. Petros had said on the excursion to the temple that a German baron, an amateur archeologist, had first stumbled on the site in the twenties. The phase of openly looting Greece had passed. The German must have hidden the marbles to retrieve later.

Now she'd learned the Nazis were after the marbles during the war. They'd somehow failed to remove them. Strange. They'd successfully looted every country in Europe. Why would they have a problem in Serros?

Alexis thought she knew.

*   *   *

Sophia and *yiayia*, bundled up in wool scarves and heavy sweaters, stood waiting on the pier. Sophia threw her arms around Alexis. "*Alexi mou*, there's never been so much excitement on this island. You were wise to stay away. They would have mobbed you."

"Who would have mobbed me?"

"The journalists," Sophia said.

"And the Serrians," *yiayia* croaked.

The three women took off in the direction of Nassos' *cafeneion*. *Yiayia* went around back to the kitchen.

Sophia peeked in the front door, beckoned to Alexis. "Michalis and Nassos are both there. Can I listen in? I won't say a word."

"Sophia *mou*, it's private, at least at the beginning."

Michalis had established himself, surrounded by little plates of *mezedakia*, at the same table where Alexis had asked him for help with her court case. He waved his bottle of *ouzo* as she came in. She waved back, looked around for Nassos, who signaled from the bar.

"The lady of the mountain." Michalis stood up and bowed.

"I'm not *the* lady, but I've seen her. Our Artemis is very beautiful."

"Just like you," he declared gallantly.

Alexis risked a joke. "There's a difference. Artemis was a virginal maiden."

Michalis guffawed. Nassos came over with a fresh bottle, his own glass, and plate of steaming cheese pies. "Made specially by Voula."

"Please thank her. And thank you for setting up this meeting."

He patted her back. "It is for us to thank you." He looked around to see if his customers needed anything. "What do you want to discuss?"

"Serros during the German occupation."

Neither man said anything.

Alexis pushed on. "I'd like to tell you what I think happened during that time. Maybe you can help me out."

Michalis shrugged. "Maybe."

It wasn't going to be easy. "When I first came to Serros, Nasso, you told me about the cave. You said the people of Serros hid there from the pirates. You didn't mention the Germans, but I suppose the people hid from them, too."

"The Germans were cruel," Nassos said.

Alexis fixed her gaze on him. "Especially when provoked." She took a deep breath. "Now, here's what I learned from Panayiotis. He said he found the marbles behind one of the stones in the base of the temple. He had a map given to him by Simeon Laurentis, who got it from a German. The German's father was in Serros during the war."

"Panayiotis told you that?" He blinked rapidly.

"Yes. This morning, in prison. Obviously, some of the German occupiers knew where the marbles were. Yet, oddly enough, they didn't take them out of Greece. Why not?"

Silence from the two men. Alexis filled their *ouzo* glasses to signal she wasn't going away. "You two were just kids during the war, but kids see things, don't they?"

Michalis heaved a sigh. "It was a long time ago. Why bring it up now?"

"Is it painful?"

His eyes surveyed the room. "We were right in what we did. We hid what happened because we didn't want the village to suffer reprisals."

"Were German soldiers killed . . . at the temple?" Alexis probed gently.

The two men stared at each other.

Alexis knew.

"Look," she said. "You're right. Why bring this up now? Let's forget this conversation."

Nassos waved his hand as if to make her wait. "They were going to loot it. We couldn't let them."

Alexis understood. Except for one thing. "You left the marbles there *after* the war?"

Nassos shrugged. "Everyone steals from Greece. They were safe there."

"Until Panayiotis." Michalis spat out the words. "You saved them, Alexi."

"You shot Panayiotis and saved my life." Only a slight exaggeration.

Michalis puffed out his chest. "I got only his leg. But I promise you one thing, Alexi. That man will never again set foot on Serros or I will kill him. I told him that at the cove. He knows I do not speak air."

Alexis had no doubt Michalis meant it. She felt a great sense of relief. "Local justice."

"You understand. You are a Serrian."

She squeezed his huge callused hand. He looked surprised, then covered her hand with his other paw.

Her eyes welled up. "My friends, do you still want to keep the secret of the temple?"

"Can *you* keep a secret?"

"I'll tell no one."

"Tell Theo. He deserves to know. You'll tell him anyway." Michalis threw back his head and roared.

"Let's swear to keep our secret," Alexis said raising her glass. "I solemnly swear."

The men crossed themselves. Then the three shook hands and emptied their glasses.

CHAPTER 23

Coming from Serros to Nemea for a few days had been a soothing balm, Alexis reflected, as she watched the afternoon sun paint the mountainside orange and red. It was close to a year since her last visit. So many changes in her life since then—the *liotrivi*, Theo, her stints as suspected murderer and antiquities sleuth, now unemployed teacher.

Helen came out to the veranda.

"You've totally spoiled me these last few days," Alexis said. "I feel so relaxed."

"Thank goodness. You were quite depressed when you got here."

"I was having a hard time with Laurentis' suicide. I kept going over the story, wanting to change the ending. Theo helped me see there are never completely happy endings. Now I'm at peace. I hope I can find the same serenity in Serros."

"You'll still be subject to some hero worship when school starts."

Alexis felt a sharp pang. "Helen, I'm not going back to Lincoln. I've been fired."

"My God. I sensed there was something more bothering you. Why didn't you say anything?"

"I didn't want to ruin the party tomorrow."

Alexis went over the scene in Hudson's office for Helen who was surprisingly phlegmatic.

"Why aren't you outraged?" Alexis said.

"It's disgusting, but I'm not surprised. Overseas schools are so afraid of jeopardizing their reputations."

"Lincoln wasn't always like that. In the old days, some of the parents demanded innovation. They even proposed I run an after-school enrichment program, but I couldn't do that and teach full time."

"Then do it now."

"How? Without Lincoln, I have no work permit."

"Get one of those parents with foreign companies to put you on the payroll. Run the after-school program for them."

Alexis cocked her head. "That's a rather creative idea. The thing is, I don't want to be one of those expatriates running around Greece, piecing together odd jobs here and there. I'm thinking of returning to the States to teach. I'll come home—I should say *back*—every summer."

"Alexis, think about what you just said, about coming home." A loud cry pierced the calm. Helen chuckled. "This baby has a ferocious appetite. Promise you won't make any rash decisions."

"I promise. Where are the girls?"

"They went somewhere with Theo. They were all being very mysterious."

Helen went off to her bedroom and came back, holding the new baby.

Alexis took his little hand. "He's perfect, but I say that with each one, don't I?"

"This one's special because he's the last. I'm naming him 'gift from God'."

Alexis' mouth dropped. "Theodoros?"

"Of course. Theo will be our *koumbaros*. I hope you'll be *koumbara*."

"First and last child. With great pleasure."

Christina burst in. "Momma! Alexi! Uncle Theo bought a house," she shrieked. "They're going to stay."

Olga ran in, jumping up and down. "I'm going to have my own room."

"Heavens. What news," Helen said, disentangling the baby's hands from her bangs.

"Alexi," Olga said, "Papa's waiting for you by the road."

She flew out the door. Theo stood leaning against a stone wall flipping through a sheaf of papers.

"The contract?" she asked.

"They told you. It was to be a surprise."

"It's an unbelievable surprise."

"I haven't signed yet. I told the owner you'd have to approve."

She grabbed his arm. "Then let's have a look."

"It's not far. In fact, the land borders a bit of Yiannis' property. I wanted Olga to be near Christina."

"And you wanted to be near your godchild."

"Ah! All the secrets have come out."

Not all, Alexis thought grimly.

They walked arm in arm down the road past a newly-planted vineyard. "There it is. That small stone house up there. I got a good price, paid for it with the reward money and a loan from Yiannis."

"What a fantastic view, Theo."

"The house needs work, but it has plumbing and electricity. Olga and I will move in right away. I need to build rooms for my parents and brother. I think I can have it ready by spring."

They climbed the dirt path.

"It has the same feeling as the *liotrivi*," Alexis said.

He beamed with pleasure, a homeowner in Greece. She'd be ten thousand miles away.

*   *   *

Theo had gone all out for his party. He grilled octopus, sausages, and chicken on the outdoor oven. The Nemea wine flowed. The party-goers feasted all Sunday afternoon on the sun-dappled veranda.

After the meal, Theo put on cassettes of plaintive Albanian music. Totally in their element, he and Olga demonstrated their village dances. Cliff and Alexis couldn't get the complicated step,

208   ELLEN BONEPARTH

but Georgia and Vaso soon whirled like gypsies to the hard-driving melodies.

Eventually, a strong evening breeze steered the company inside. Alexis took Christina and Olga, now best of friends, upstairs to bed.

"Alexi, if you move to Nemea, we can be together like this all the time," Olga said softly.

Alexis dodged. "It was a wonderful party, wasn't it?"

"She means if you marry Theo," Christina translated.

Alexis leaned over as if to strangle her. "You are half-godchild, half-brat." She pulled up the quilt. "Theo has to get the new house ready. I'll be coming to Nemea some weekends this fall, and I hope you'll both visit me in Serros." She kissed each girl. "Now whisper all night long."

In the living room, the Athens contingent was collecting its things. Yiannis, holding the baby, got up from his armchair, yawning. "Four more days and the harvest will be done."

"Speaking of harvests," Georgia said, "I have a small announcement. Helen, can we have a last sip of wine?"

Helen circled the group, filling everyone's glass. "This time, next year, it will be a fine red."

"I'll bring the olives." Georgia looked mischievously at Alexis. "I should have a large store by then."

Alexis gaped. "You didn't."

"I most certainly did."

"I don't believe it."

"I did it. Finally. I'm so excited."

"What in God's name are you two talking about?" Vaso asked.

Cliff held out his glass in a toast. "It's obvious. Georgia did something outrageous as usual. Here's to it, whatever it is."

Yiannis cracked up. Helen pulled on his arm. "What is it? Do you know?"

"Honestly, I don't."

Helen fixed her gaze on Theo who reddened. "Do you?"

"He's part of it," Georgia said. "We just have to get Alexis to agree."

The company looked around at each other, still baffled.

"End of mystery," Georgia said. "I am to be a citizen of Serros. I'm finished with Sounion."

"Serros?" Vaso repeated, obviously appalled Georgia would exchange Sounion for Serros.

"A dream place," Georgia replied. "Nitsa came to me last week, begging to sell the Koutsos properties. She has power of attorney for Panayiotis. They're obviously desperate—the price was ridiculously low. Being a terrible romantic *and* a shrewd businesswoman, I bought both pieces."

Georgia winked at Theo. "Theo will build me a stone house on Loukas' land, assuming Alexis approves."

Alexis exploded with joy—Georgia becoming her neighbor, Theo building Georgia's house. She frowned, tried to look serious. "I have no objection as long as you two promise not to obstruct my view."

Georgia clucked her tongue. "I was thinking of a tower, but we can negotiate."

Alexis threw up her hands. "Neighbors. Again."

Everyone roared.

Alexis felt a tug on her heart seeing in her mind the *liotrivi*, the olive orchards, the view from her kitchen window. It was time to go home. "Now, I also have an announcement. I am no longer in the employ of the Lincoln School."

"It's true," Vaso screeched. "Alexi, I heard a rumor but didn't believe it."

"No, it's true. I've been fired. I'm not sure whether to make a stink or go quietly. I need to consult with you and Cliff about that."

Cliff came over, put his arm around her. "You got a crappy deal. What next, Alexi?"

"I'd pretty much decided to give up, go back to America."

At that, Theo leaned forward, his head in his hands.

She needed to end his misery quickly. "But that isn't what I want. Helen helped me see my home is here. It *is* here. Hudson can fire me, but he can't uproot me."

Theo looked up, ran his fingers through his hair, exhaled deeply.

"What will you do?" Vaso said.

"I'm going to try innovative after-school programs, maybe even a summer camp in Nemea or Serros."

"There's my new house," Georgia said. "Perhaps Theo would hire you to stain and varnish."

"Before you all overemploy me, I want to say something else." Alexis gazed around her circle. "I learned a lot this year—how to restore a house, bluff my way through some interesting situations, care for people and . . . how to let them care for me." She swallowed. "Damn. This is coming out too sentimental."

"So what?" Cliff said.

"Okay. The main thing I learned is I can't do it alone. The olive press taught me that. The people who harassed me, the people who helped me—well, the world's full of both. You can't build your dream house and live in a dream. You can't find the perfect school, or island, or country. You find the people who matter and build your life with them."

Yiannis, still holding the baby, moved over to Helen, his free arm around her neck. "Truth, Alexi. Sometimes you find them in the strangest places. I remember this beautiful woman turning up one day on a dig, smeared with dust, sweating like a pig. What a love story."

Laughing, Alexis looked across at Theo. "I've got one, too."